First Edition
If Houses Could Talk
2015

Mountain Top Books

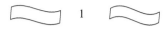

1

Published by Mountain Top Books

A division of Foundation for Publication

3516 Kelvin Avenue Fort Worth, Texas 76133

 2

IF HOUSES COULD TALK
OH THE STORIES THEY WOULD TELL

By Lela Suttee

IF HOUSES COULD TALK

By Lela Suttee

© 2014

If houses could talk, oh the stories they would tell

of the people who live there

their happiness, their hell.

The paint on the wall would certainly convey

whether their lives were colorful

or dismal gray.

Would the chandelier shine within its room

or would it be darkened because of their gloom?

The water that remains on the window pane,

is it their tears or last night's rain?

Would it love its owner, or have disdain?

Would it be happy, or sad that they remain?

Are their stories one it would tell or keep hidden within its shell?

Only the house could truthfully say, what went on in it's rooms of the many yesterdays.

 4

Dedication

I dedicate this book to my beloved mother, Priscilla Defoor Suttee for instilling in me the love of all things old.

Acknowledgments

I would like to acknowledge the help given to me in bringing this book to life. For their patience and guidance I wish to thank Mae Hoover, Carla Coffee and my husband Ray Jackson who believed in me even when I didn't believe in myself.

I would also like to thank Madison Hoover for the design of my book cover.

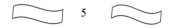

STORY ONE

ELIJAH

Elijah's house

[Ouch!] Those kids are throwing rocks at me again, you'd think they'd know better. This neighborhood was once occupied by honest hard-working folks who taught their kids how to behave. Their homes were well taken care of and their yards were pristine. Children were safe to play outside, and police sirens were rarely heard.

This is a stark contrast to what I see around me today. Many families have moved out of the neighborhood. Crime is up and now this is considered the poor side of town. Homes are frequently vandalized and I'm no exception. I'm a mere shell of the house I used to be. My paint is chipping, some of my windows are broken, and I'm in bad need of a new roof.

The man that lives within my walls is sick and can barely get around. The only company he has is the nurse that comes to take care of him each day. He, too, is a shell of the man he used to be. When he was young he was a strong hard-working man. He built me with his own two hands. His name is Elijah Sims and I'm proud to be his home.

The children that throw rocks at me don't come very close. I overheard one of them say, "Don't get too close. A crazy man lives there! He likes to hang out at the graveyard. "

You see, for years Elijah would walk to the graveyard everyday. He would stay hours in front of one particular grave, that of his beloved Sarah. Other than that he wasn't seen much except on occasion to buy food and supplies. He couldn't work anymore due to an injury he got on the job. He lives on a small pension. He's a broken man and most people don't know why. However the mayor does, but he's not talking.

So let's venture back in time to the beginning of my story.

Oh, how I know this story so well. For I have heard it many times. Elijah would tell it to his nurse and each time he would think he was telling her for the first time.

Elijah was 18 years old when he first saw Sarah. She came with her father to the lumberyard where Elijah worked. He couldn't help but smile as he watched her interact with her father. Her eyes glistened when she smiled. Her hair was fiery red and her eyes were as green as emeralds. His heart seemed to stop when she walked by and smiled. He knew then and there he had to meet her.

To his dismay he found out she was a Taylor. The Taylor's were one of the richest families in town. Eric Taylor owned a big law firm. His wife Sadie had inherited her father's oil company when he died. So one might say they were set for life. Sarah was their only daughter and they had high hopes for her. This would not include Elijah, a mere commoner.

They had another man in mind. His name was Winston Cargill. He was being raised by his father Jackson Cargill, who was the Mayor of our town. Jackson had lost his wife to cancer when Winston was just five years old. Winston had many "mothers" but none of them ever stayed around very long. So to compensate Jackson spoiled him. He was very wealthy and he spared nothing when it came to his son.

Winston was 18 at the time, and from what I've heard quite good-looking, and he knew it. He definitely had his father's ego. He was quite popular with the girls, but he wanted Sarah Taylor. However that didn't stop him from stealing kisses from his many admirers. The word womanizer comes to mind. Yet their fathers made it quite clear they wanted him and Sarah together.

However Elijah was just stubborn enough that he wasn't going to let that deter him. It wasn't long before an opportunity knocked. When Sarah and her father were in the store he ordered a bunch of lumber. It was to be delivered that Friday. Elijah readily volunteered to do the job.

When he arrived no one was home. So he started unloading the lumber in front of the garage as instructed. Although he was disappointed he decided to work slowly in the hope she would come home before he was through.

He about fell off his truck when he heard a voice behind him.

"You need some help?"

After composing himself he turned around. There was Sarah smiling up at him.

"You okay?" she said with a slight giggle.

"I just wasn't expecting anyone," he said as he took off his hat in respect.

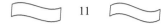

"I'm Sarah," *she said as she grabbed a board.*

"It's nice to meet you, Sarah. I am Elijah".

"I haven't seen you before. Are you new in town?"

"Yes, my parents and I moved here last summer.
My dad is in the oilfield and we move around a lot."

"I've been here my whole life," *she said as she lay
down the board on the stack.*

"This seems to be a nice little town. The people
seem really friendly."

"Yes, that's true. We are quite friendly, but there's
not a lot to do around here. It's a bit boring.
However, I think it's about to get a little more
interesting," *she said as she looked up at Elijah and
smiled.*

"Yes, maybe so," *he said, smiling back.*

"How about I show you around town and introduce
you to some of my friends?"

"That sounds nice, but I better get back to the store before I get fired."

"Meet me at Buddy's tomorrow at noon. It's downtown on the square."

"Okay see you tomorrow."

When Elijah was on his way back to the store he was grinning from ear to ear. All afternoon all he could think about was Sarah. What would he wear and what would he talk about. He didn't want to look stupid in front of her or her friends. However he didn't want to put on airs. That just wasn't Elijah's way. Later that evening he was having dinner with his parents. His mother could tell he had something on his mind. He was more quiet than usual and he didn't seem to have an appetite.

"Elijah, did something happen today"?

"Yes ma'am, I met a girl. Her name is Sarah Taylor and she is as nice as she is pretty".

"Well then, what's seems to be the problem?"

"Her family is very rich, and she's quite popular. She offered to show me around town and introduce me to some of her friends. You know me, Mom, I'm a bit shy. So I'm worried about what she and her friends will think of me."

Like always his mother put his worries to rest. "Elijah Sims, you just be yourself! If she is the right one it will all work out."

His father just patted him on the back and said, " It'll be all right, Son."

They always knew how to make him feel better.

Daniel Sims was an oil driller. He worked seven days a week at times. He was a man of few words. However when he spoke, you can bet it was something important. Beth Sims was the talker of the family. She'd love to tell stories. Her laugh was contagious. If you were around Beth you were laughing. She could make anyone who was sad feel better. Elijah loved them both dearly. He's always talking about them to the nurse who cares for him. He repeats the same stories over and over, but she is patient and just sits and listens.

Now back to my story

It was about 11 o'clock the next morning and Elijah was so nervous that he cut himself while shaving. He tried on several shirts before he finally decided on the blue one. He ironed it and quickly got dressed. He kissed his mama goodbye and grabbed his hat as he went out the door.

All the way to town he kept saying "Elijah, just don't say something stupid."

It was a beautiful spring day. He rolled down the window to get some fresh air. He took a deep breath, while his mother's words danced in his head.

"Elijah Sims, just be your self and if she is the right one it will all work out."

He found himself smiling as he reached town. When he got to the square he spotted Buddy's and there was Sarah waiting for him at the front entrance.

He parked his truck across the Street at the courthouse, for there were no parking spots in front of Buddy's. When he was approaching Sarah he could see that she was smiling.

He smiled back and said, "So this is where you hang out on a Saturday afternoon."

"Yes, and wait till you try their milkshakes. They are the best!"

So he opened the door for her and they went in. She thought it was so sweet and kindly said, "Thank you".

Although Elijah said, "You're welcome", *he thought to himself,* "isn't that the way a gentleman treats a lady?"

Oh, this takes me back to one of the many times that Elijah was telling the nurse his story. Elijah always started off his story with, "I remember like it was yesterday."

What prompted him to tell the story was the nurse complained about how unkind one of her male patients had been. He went on and on about how a lady should be treated. Then he told about his first date with Sarah including every detail about how he showed Sarah the respect that a lady deserves.

But I digress.

Sarah directed him to a booth at the back of the Café and they sat down. Before he could collect his thoughts and say anything the waitress appeared.

"What can I get you two?"

"I would like a chocolate milkshake, please."

"How about you, cowboy?"

"I'll take strawberry."

"Will that be all?"

"Yes, thank you."

When the waitress left, Sarah said "Elijah, tell me a little bit about yourself."

Elijah began with "Well I was born in the little town of Pecos Texas. I am an only child. We have moved around a lot due to my father working in the oilfield. I had to change schools often but I finally graduated last year. "

"It was exciting moving around at first but now I'm ready to put down some roots."

"So if your dad gets transferred again, will you follow?"

"I'm not sure. But enough about me. Tell me about yourself."

Elijah never liked talking about himself much.

Sarah was about to tell him her story when Winston showed up at Buddy's.

Sarah motioned for him to come over and meet Elijah.

She began introducing him only to be interrupted by Winston.

"Oh yeah, your family is renting my uncle's old house that he usually uses for his hired hands. How's that working out for you Elijah?"

"It's just fine. Mr. Cargill has been really good to us."

"Well, good for you, Elijah," *he said as he patted him on the back.* "Guess I'll see you around. I better get back to my friends. I don't want them to think I'm being rude."

Sarah was sitting there with her mouth wide open.

"I'm so sorry, Elijah. He was really rude."

"Oh that's okay. You don't need to apologize. I'm used to his kind."

Sarah got up to confront him.

Elijah took her arm very gently and said, "Don't bother. It's not worth it."

So she sat back down.

"You were saying?"

"Well, I'm graduating this year. I was born and raised here in Parker Valley. I, too, am an only child. My dad is a lawyer and my mom runs the family oil company. After I graduate they want me to take some business courses so I can help Mom with her company."

"Is that what you want to do?"

"I'm not sure but I would hate to disappoint my parents."

"Oh, I'm sure they would understand if you had a different interest. Most parents just want their children to be happy."

"Well, my father is a bit of a control freak. In fact, if he could pick my husband he would."

Elijah just laughed and said, "Oh surely not."

After visiting a little longer they decided to go for a drive. Sarah showed him some of the points of interest around town. She began with the local library.

"That's where I spent many an evening doing research for the countless essays and reports."

"Oh, I bet you miss that."

"Yeah right," *She said sarcastically.* "Over there is our little theater. My friends and I had a lot of good times there. It seems the whole world saw the movies way before we did, but we enjoyed them nonetheless."

"It was the same in a lot of the little towns we lived in. Maybe we can go to the movie sometime?"

"I would like that. Hey turn here and I'll show you the pool. It will open sometime next month. This is where I spent most of my summers. However, now that school is almost over there won't be much time for swimming."

"Oh, I'm sure there will be some time."

"Maybe so."

"You seem to be sad about graduating."

"Well, it's just a little scary. having to decide about your future, making the right choices, becoming an adult. It's a bit daunting."

"Don't let it worry you. It will all come together and you will be fine."

"I hope you're right. Hey let me take you to a place I love to go when I need some time alone."

"Show me the way." *They headed down Main Street and Sarah pointed out one last point of interest.*

"That is Bill's Steakhouse. Their steak is really good. You've got to try it."

"Sounds good."

When leaving town they passed the local graveyard.

"That's where my favorite grandparents are buried. "I sure do miss them."

"How long have they been gone?"

"Its been about five years, but there's still a hole in my heart."

"I'm sorry for your loss."

"Thanks, it's just they seemed to understand me better than even my parents do. They did just want me to be happy."

"Yeah, grandparents are good that way."

"Are your grandparents still alive, Elijah?"

"No, they are all gone."

"Sorry."

Then there was silence. It wasn't an awkward silence. It was like they both knew it was a moment to reflect. Sarah motioned for Elijah to turn left. They went quite a ways down a winding dirt road. It was definitely off the beaten path. Then Sarah had him turn right. There laid before him was some of the most beautiful land Elijah had ever seen.

The whole place was covered with bluebonnets. There were trees everywhere. In a clearing Elijah could see a tank. It was full that time of the year because of the spring rains. Down by the tank was an old wooden bench. So they decided to sit a spell and take it all in.

"It sure is beautiful here."

"Yeah, I love this place."

All of a sudden a gust of wind caught Elijah's hat and he and Sarah began the chase. It kept getting out of their reach, but they laughed and continued anyway. It finally stopped for a minute and they both went for it and ended up falling. Elijah jumped up and offered his hand to help Sarah up. As he pulled her up, they were very close.

She looked deeply into his eyes and said, "Elijah Sims, you are quite the gentleman." *She then kissed him gently on the cheek.*

He smiled sheepishly and said, "Well I was worried that you had hurt yourself."

"No, I'm fine. If anything is bruised it's my ego."

24

They went back to the bench and talked a while. It was obvious they enjoyed each other's company. It seemed like they had known each other forever.

The sun was coming down and the view was beautiful. It was the kind of sunset that would take your breath away.

Elijah, being the gentleman he was, suggested that they better head back before it got dark.

On the way back to town he asked, "May I see you again?"

She said, "I would like that." *It was almost dark when they got back. She thanked him again and got out of the truck.*

"See you soon."

"Not if I see you before."

He heard her laugh as she got in her car. He waited to see if her car started. When she was on her way, he headed home.

BACK TO THE PRESENT

"OH NO! Elijah just fell. The nurse is running to him. It's a good thing she's here."

"Mr. Sims, are you okay."

"I think so. Just please help me up."

"Does anything hurt?"

"No."

"Walk with me a bit. I want to make sure you didn't break anything."

"Okay."

"You sure you're okay?"

"Yeah, I think I'm fine."

*"The nurse is helping him back to his chair now. I'm
sure glad he's okay,"*

"How about some tea, Mr. Sims?"

"That would be nice. Thank you."

"Oh by the way, you can call me Elijah."

"Okay, Elijah it is."

*"She is such a sweet and caring person. I'm so
glad she's here to take care of Elijah. It takes
someone special to be a nurse. Elsa Thomas is
that special person. She has devoted her whole life
to helping the elderly.*

*She is so tender and kind to Elijah. Although she
has many things to tend to, she's willing to sit a
spell, and listen to Elijah's stories."*

*"Oh yeah, that reminds me. I bet you want me to get
back to the story."*

When Elijah arrived home his parents were anxious to hear about his day. He sat down on the couch and said "Mom, Dad, is there really such a thing as love at first sight?"

"Well son, I knew I wanted to marry your mother the first time I saw her."

Elijah's mother patted her husband on the back and said "Oh Daniel, you're such a sweetheart."

Then she turned to Elijah and asked "What's she like son?"

"Well she is really down to earth. Although her family is rich she doesn't act like she's better than me. She's very friendly and outgoing. It's so easy to talk to her. I really enjoyed her company. She showed me around town and then she took me to see some of the prettiest land I have ever seen."

"Well it seems you had a good time, Son."

"Yes, I really did."

Across town Sarah's parents were waiting for her as well. However they weren't as happy to hear about her day with Elijah.

Her dad started with "What are you doing running around with the likes of Elijah Sims?"

"I didn't know you were so concerned about who I choose to run around with."

"Sarah, he can't give you what you're accustomed to."

"What exactly would that be Dad?"

"You know the nice things that someone of means can give you. For instance like Winston Cargill. I thought you liked him."

"No Dad, you like him. I think he is a complete snob. Was he the one that told you about Elijah?"

"Yes, but nonetheless you can't see Elijah any more."

"Dad I'm almost 18. Shouldn't I have the choice of who I run around with?"

"Young lady, you are 17 and under my roof. You haven't even finished school yet. You will not see him again and that's final."

Sarah ran up stairs and slammed her bedroom door behind her.

After looking at her husband with great displeasure Sadie quickly left the room to go console her daughter.

From listening to Elijah I got the feeling that Sadie was a very loving, hands-on mother.

She made it a point to be there for her daughter. She regretted not being able to have more children. So she showered Sarah with all her love.

When Sarah was older and didn't need her mother as much, Sadie found another way to fulfill that motherly need. She started a garden club for the children in the neighborhood. Once a week she would have them over to teach them about all the various plants and how to keep them healthy.

Each child was given their own plant to take care of. She always had a pitcher of fresh lemonade and cookies for them. They just loved her.

"Oops I went off on a tangent again. Sorry".

Sarah was lying on the bed crying when her mother came into the room. She sat down beside her and gently brushed her hair back from her face.

"Oh honey, don't cry. Your dad means well. He wants the best for you. He just doesn't have a way with words."

"Mom, should I not have the choice of whom I associate with? Elijah is a very nice person. Y'all are judging him on the basis of how much money he has. Money doesn't make a person who they are."

"That is true, dear, but it does make a difference of how well he can provide for you."

"Mom, we just met. We're just friends."

"Your father and I know that. However we know where this could lead. We just want to make sure you find a man that can take good care of you."

"He wants to put a stop to this before it gets started."

"It's not fair. You and dad don't even know Elijah."

"I know, honey. I will talk to your father. However I doubt it will do any good. Now come and eat your dinner."

The next day Elijah decided to pay Sarah a visit. Although he didn't know what happened the night before he nervously knocked on the door. Sarah and her mother were out grocery shopping. So guess who came to the door. Eric opened the door and saw Elijah standing there and immediately frowned.

"Hello Sir, my name is Elijah Sims." Elijah held out his hand to shake Eric's.

Without extending his hand in return he said, "Yes, and how can I help you?"

"Well sir, I was hoping to talk to Sarah."

"Sarah is out shopping with her mother.

Did Sarah tell you that she already has a boyfriend?"

"No sir. I was not aware of that."

"Well, it's best if you don't come around here anymore."

Elijah held back his sadness and said, "Alright Sir. I'm sorry I bothered you. You have a nice day."

Elijah got back in his truck and drove off.

Just as he rounded the corner, here came Sarah and her mother. Sarah quickly got out of the car to stop Elijah but he didn't see her and kept going. She ran into the house to ask her dad what Elijah said.

"Well he wanted to see you. However I told him you were seeing someone else and not to come around here anymore."

"You lied to him. You know I'm not seeing anybody else."

Then Sarah ran out of the room once again crying. Later that night, Sarah made a call to her best friend Jenny.

"Hey Jen, it's Sarah."

"Hey girl, what's going on?"

"Elijah came to see me today and Dad ran him off. He had the nerve to tell him I already had a boyfriend."

"Oh, that's not good."

"Now, Elijah's never going to want to talk to me again."

"He will understand when you tell him the truth."

"That's just it. My dad is going to be watching me really close. Also that snob Winston Cargill will tell on me if he sees me with Elijah."

"I'm sorry Sarah. Is there anything I can do?"

"Yeah, tomorrow I want you to go to the lumberyard and tell Elijah what happened. Tell him I would like to meet him on Saturday at the land that I showed him. Find out what time he can meet me and let me know."

"Sure. I'll call you tomorrow about what he says."

"Thanks so much."

"You're welcome, that's what friends are for."

"I love you, Jen!"

"I Love you too. So what's he like? He must be pretty special for you to go against your dad."

"Yeah he is. I've never felt like this before. It's like we've known each other forever."

Sarah heard a knock at her door. "I've got to go. Someone is at the door. See you later. Bye".

"Bye."

Sarah quickly put down the phone and laid-back just as her mother opened the door. "Sarah, are you okay? You're up quite late."

"Oh I'm fine. I was just finishing up some homework."

Sarah's mother came over and sat down.

"I'm sorry for how it went today with your father. You know how stubborn he can be. He's just looking out for his little girl."

"I know Mom. It's just that he doesn't even know Elijah and yet he thinks he's bad for me. He didn't even give him a chance."

"Well don't worry, things will cool off and we can address it then."

"Maybe so."

Her mother gently kissed her on the cheek and said, "I love you, my daughter."

36

Sarah smiled and said, "Love you too, Mom."

After her mother left the room, Sarah laid back down and reflected on her time with Elijah. She found herself smiling as she drifted off to sleep.

Across town Elijah laid in his bed saddened by the day's events. He really wanted to see Sarah again, but he didn't know how or if she wanted to see him.

"She could've told me she had a boyfriend. I thought she really liked me. I feel like such a fool. Why would someone like her be interested in someone like me anyway?"

He had to work the next morning so he desperately tried to go to sleep. However he tossed and turned all night.

The next morning his alarm went off at 7 o'clock as usual. Elijah found it difficult to get up. Nonetheless he dragged himself out of bed. He managed to get himself ready and headed to work.

All day he tried really hard to keep his focus on the job. However he couldn't help but think about Sarah and how much he enjoyed being with her.

Later that afternoon Elijah was unloading the supply truck when Jenny showed up. She stood there a while just watching him. She couldn't help but notice his tanned muscular arms. He is quite handsome, she thought to herself. It's no wonder Sarah is attracted to him.

"Excuse me, are you Elijah?"

"Yes, how can I help you?" *he said as he continued to unload the truck.*

"I'm Jenny, Sarah's friend."

Elijah stopped cold. He turned around to face Jenny.

"She asked me to come and tell you that her dad lied to you. She is not seeing anyone else. He just doesn't want her to see you. He is watching her like a hawk. So she wants to meet you this Saturday at the land that she showed you the other day. She wants to know what would be a good time for you."

"I get off work at 6 o'clock. I could meet her about 6:30."

"That's great! I'll let her know."

Elijah was thrilled that Sarah wanted to see him again. He was anxious to hear what she had to say. The rest of the week seemed to drag on forever.

Saturday finally came and Elijah was as nervous as a cat on my hot tin roof. 6 o'clock couldn't come fast enough. When he finally got off work, he rushed home to clean up a bit before meeting Sarah.

His trip there was uneventful other then the mama cow that got in his way. However she eventually moved on after he honked his horn several times.

Elijah is very detailed when he tells the story to Elsa his nurse.

When he finally arrived Sarah wasn't there yet so he sat down on the bench to enjoy the scenery. It was a beautiful spring evening. The temperature was mild and there was a nice breeze. He took a brief moment to say a prayer. When he finished Sarah had arrived.

"Hi."

"Hi."

"Elijah, I just want to apologize for how my father treated you. I told you he was a control freak."

Elijah took her hand and said, "It's all right. He feels like he's protecting you."

Sarah sat down and sighed.

"He thinks I would be better off with that snob Winston Cargill. He's probably having him keep tabs on me."

"How does your mother feel about you seeing me?"

"She's been supporting me through the whole thing. She came in my room the other night to comfort me. However she has very little say. My father says 'my house my rules.'"

"I can see you and your mother are very close."

"Yeah she's awesome! I can always count on her to be there for me. She's such a good mother. She always wanted more children but she couldn't have any more."

"I'm so sorry."

"She has managed to find other ways to fill that need. Just last week she started a garden club for the children in the neighborhood. They each have their own plant to take care of. Then after that they get to feast on homemade cookies and freshly squeezed lemonade."

"That's so nice of her."

"Yeah, she's really good that way."

"So, Sarah, where does that leave you and me?"

"Well, we will just have to sneak around. How about we meet out here every chance we get? We could maybe have a picnic next time."

"That sounds nice."

That very day a friendship started between them that wouldn't be easily shaken. Sarah had told her mom she was spending the night with Jenny. So they talked into the wee hours of the night. Elijah found it so easy to talk to Sarah. It was apparent to him that she felt the same way.

Later that night before they said their goodbyes, Elijah shyly looked at Sarah and said, "Do you mind if I kiss you?"

Before he could even finish the sentence, Sarah wrapped her arms around him and gave him a kiss he wouldn't soon forget.

They tried to see each other as much as possible, even if it was only for an hour. Elijah treasured every moment he could spend with Sarah.

It was amongst those trees and bluebonnets, sitting on that wooden bench, that Elijah and Sarah fell in love. They talked about their hopes and dreams. They soon realized that they had one particular hope in common, that they could be together without having to hide.

Although Elijah and Sarah couldn't be seen together, he made sure he saw her walk across the stage and get her diploma.

He slipped in after everyone was seated. He stayed in the back of the auditorium. Then after Sarah accepted her diploma he slipped out without anyone seeing him.

Elijah's favorite story to tell was when he told Sarah for the first time that he was in love with her. She had brought his favorite lunch. Cold fried chicken and potato salad. Heavy on the pickles. He would rant and rave over the fresh squeezed lemonade she would bring.

He was very nervous because he didn't know how she would react, so he took a deep breath and just blurted it out.

"Sarah Taylor, I'm in love with you!"

Elijah had told Elsa his nurse that he found her reaction very sweet.

"I know, silly, and I feel the same way about you."

About that time George Jones came on the truck radio, Elijah jumped up and said "My lady, would you like to dance?" *and then extended his hand.*

"Why, kind sir, I believe I would."

Elijah took her in his arms and they danced. When the song was over Elijah drew her close to him and kissed her tenderly on the lips. They were both very much in love. It was truly the happiest time of their lives.

When Elijah got home that evening his father was waiting for him.

"Son, there's something I must tell you. I know you are quite smitten with Sarah."

"Yes Sir. I am."

'I'm sorry to have to tell you this. My job here is almost finished and we already have a new location to go to. So we will be leaving in a month."

"Dad, I can't go with you."

"I know, Son. However you are going to need a place to live. So I took some of my savings and I bought you a plot of land. It is in a new neighborhood they are developing."

Mr. Cargill says you can stay here while you build your house. He says he needs some help around the farm."

By this time tears were rolling down Elijah's face. He hugged his dad and said, "I'm going to miss you and Mom a lot."

"Well Son, this is an opportunity for you to prove to Mr. Taylor that you can take care of his daughter."

"Thank you so much, Dad."

About that time Elijah's mother appeared. She gave her son a hug and said, "I love you, my son, and I hope all your dreams come true."

That last few weeks before his parents moved, Elijah and his father prepared the land for me and built my foundation. I had to be up to code, so when the inspector came he gave me a thumbs up. So I was well on my way to becoming Elijah and Sarah's home.

The day came for his parents to leave. It was a sad time for all of them. Beth was quite emotional and didn't want to let Elijah go.

Daniel didn't let his emotions show for he felt he had to be the strong one. He hugged his son and said. "Come on, Hon, We got to get on the road.

Elijah stood there waving tlll their car was out of sight. He had never felt so alone. The only thing that lessened his pain was that he would see Sarah later that evening.

Elijah went to the lumberyard to purchase the wood to start framing up my walls. He didn't want to tell Sarah about me until he had me dried in. I felt honored that I was his gift to Sarah. He planned to ask for her hand in marriage when he presented me to her. He hoped it would be a magical moment.

Later that evening he met Sarah at the land. She apologized for being late. She had stopped at Jenny's for a while because she thought she was being followed. Elijah was just so glad to see her. He took her in his arms and kissed her. She could feel his desperation.

"Are you okay?"

"I'm going to miss my parents a lot! I've never had to be without them."

"I'm sorry, Elijah."

"Don't be. I would do anything to be with you."

Sarah put her arms around Elijah's waist and laid her head against his chest. "I'm glad to hear that because I would do anything to be with you, too."

Elijah kissed her on her head and held her very tight.

"My parents really liked you."

"Oh I liked them too. I thought it was so cool how they were willing to hide out with us. Your mom is so sweet. Your dad is such a gentleman. You two are a lot alike, you know."

"Oh I don't know about that, but I would like to think so. My dad is a real good man."

"So are you Elijah, and don't you forget it."

Some clouds had rolled in and it began to rain. It was raining pretty hard, so they got in Elijah's truck.

BACK TO THE PRESENT

Speaking of rain, it's raining here, but that's not my biggest problem. It's hailing as well and that's not helping my already damaged roof. Elijah is lying on his bed staring out the window. He's not feeling well tonight. In fact he's been under the weather for a good two weeks now. I hope he gets to feeling better real soon. However I don't think Elijah believes he will.

He had a lawyer over today to write up his will. He's giving everything to Elsa. She has been so good to him. Lately she has even stayed overnight to care for Elijah. He loves her for that, and the fact she is always up for one of his stories.

OH YEAH BACK TO THE STORY

The rain had lightened. So they got out of the truck. Elijah asked Sarah if she would like to dance. Without saying a word she extended her hand. Although they were getting wet, they didn't seem to care. They were together and that's all that mattered.

Several months passed. All the while Elijah continued working on me, working for Mr. Cargill, and working at the lumberyard. At times he was very tired, but he never missed an opportunity to see Sarah.

One evening when they were sitting on the bench, Elijah fell asleep on Sarah's shoulder. She just let him sleep. When Elijah woke up, he felt so embarrassed. He told Elsa he turned bright red. She just laughed and laughed. For the most part she seemed to enjoy Elijah's stories. However there were times when she would excuse herself. I would hear her crying in the kitchen.

I can tell she really cares for Elijah. Just the other day when he was still feeling pretty bad Elsa served him breakfast in bed. Then she sat down beside him and asked him to tell her about the day he proposed to Sarah. Although she had heard the story many times, she knew it was his favorite. He seemed to light up when he would tell it.

He started with, "I remember like it was yesterday. I had finally gotten the house dried in. Sarah and I had planned to meet later that evening. So when she arrived I told her I had something to show her. I didn't want her to be recognized when we went to town. So I had bought her a hat and a pair of sunglasses at the dime store. She thought she looked ridiculous.

Elijah chuckled at this point and said, "But I thought she was as cute as a bug's ear. I stopped a couple of blocks away from the house to blindfold her. Then when we arrived, I led her into the house. I got down on one knee and told her to take off the blindfold."

"Sarah Taylor. I'm crazy in love with you. I can't imagine my life without you. So I've been building this house so I could show your father that I can take care of you. Will you make me the happiest man on earth and marry me?"

"I can still see her standing there with tears running down her face. 'Yes, yes, I will marry you.' "

"We just held each other tight and cried together."

Elijah began tearing up.

Elsa handed him a tissue and said, "Don't cry Elijah, you will see Sarah again."

Elijah took her hand and patted it. "You're a good woman, Elsa, and I'm so glad to have you as my nurse, and my friend. I appreciate how well you take care of me. "

It's nice of you to humor an old man by listening to his stories. "

"I love listening to your stories, Elijah. Now you get some rest and I'll come and check on you later."

I really love Elsa. I'm so glad Elijah is giving me to her. I hope I can be a comfortable home for her for many years to come. Elijah is helping Elsa more than he knows. You see, the other day I overheard her talking on the telephone to a friend. She was bemoaning the fact that her marriage was over. She caught her husband Sam with another woman. She was really worried about where she would go when the divorce was final. She told her friend that there's no way she could afford to live in the house she lives in now.

Speaking of houses, after Elijah's proposal was accepted he wanted to finish me as soon as possible. He worked on me every chance he got. Sometimes he would work late into the night. He didn't want to marry Sarah until he had finished me. However that never happened. You see, before I was completely done tragedy struck.

Remember when Sarah was worried that she was being followed? Well she had reason to be. Winston was following her that day. When he thought she was only going to Jenny's he left.

However, it wasn't long before he caught Sarah and Elijah together. Although he didn't confront them at the time he wasn't going to let it go.

The very next day he went to the lumberyard. He told Elijah that he had been following Sarah and knew their little secret. He warned him if he continued to see Sarah he would tell her father. He even had the gall to tell Elijah that if he really loved Sarah he would let her go. So that she could marry someone that could take better care of her.

Elijah and Sarah were supposed to meet later that evening. So he planned to tell her about Winston's visit. Then they would go together and talk to her father. However, Sarah never showed up. He was really worried so he went to her house. Sarah's car was in the driveway but when he knocked on the door no one answered. He figured that she must've gone somewhere with her parents. So then he headed home.

When he got to work the next day, his boss called him into his office. He knew that Elijah and Sarah were seeing each other secretly.

But he never told a soul.

He asked Elijah to sit down because he had some bad news for him. His next words sent chills down Elijah's spine.

"Sarah accidentally fell down her stairs yesterday.

The fall broke her neck. I'm sorry Elijah, but Sarah's dead. Winston Cargill was with her when it happened. He's pretty broke up about it."

Elijah's world was turned upside down that day. He's never been the same. When he was telling the story to Elsa he said that he didn't believe that it was an accident. He knew in his heart that Winston had pushed her down those stairs. He also told her that it makes him sick how Winston sits up there in his office playing Mayor all the while he is a cold blooded murderer. To this day he bemoans the fact that he has no way to prove it.

BACK TO THE PRESENT

Elsa was here bright and early this morning. She's in the kitchen preparing breakfast now.

Oh, Elijah must be awake. He's calling for her.

"Did you have a good night's rest, Elijah?"

"Yes I did. Thank you."

"Breakfast is almost ready. Would you like some coffee?"

"Yes, that would be nice."

When Elsa returns with the coffee, she sits down beside him. "I was wondering if you would like to go to the graveyard and put fresh flowers on Sarah's grave?"

"I would like that very much. That is very kind of you. I'm getting weaker and I don't know how much longer I have before I won't be able to go anymore."

"Hopefully that's not the case. However it's a beautiful sunny day outside. So I thought you might enjoy getting out of the house for a few hours."

"Thank you so much, Elsa."

"Okay, you get dressed. I'll finish breakfast."

54

Elijah is crying now. This is happening more and more these days. I can tell he still grieves over the fact that Winston Cargill is getting away with murder. Oh that reminds me of a time when Elijah confronted Winston about Sarah's death. I can quote it almost word for word because Elijah has repeated that story many many times to Elsa.

Elijah would go to Buddies and sit in the booth where he and Sarah sat on their first date. He said it made him feel closer to Sarah. He would order a strawberry milkshake and just sit and reminisce about their time together.

On one of these occasions Winston showed up. When he saw Elijah he turned around and headed out the door. Elijah jumped up and followed him outside.

"I know you killed her."

"Oh, you do, do you."

"I don't think it's a coincidence that the very day you tell me to stop seeing her, she ends up at the bottom of the stairs. And it's while you're with her."

"That's quite a story, too bad you can't prove it."

When Winston started to walk off he stopped and turned around and said. "Oh, by the way, I saw that little house you built. Hope you enjoy living in it alone."

Elijah said he came very close to hitting Winston that day. However he realized it wasn't the Christian thing to do, nor would it bring Sarah back.

After Sarah's death he couldn't bring himself to court any other woman. The few dates he did go on, didn't turn out that well. He found himself always comparing them to Sarah. Then he had the accident on the job and had to go on disability. It was then that he decided never to marry. He didn't feel he could provide well enough for a family. It's such a shame because he would've made a very good husband and father. Life is cruel sometimes. It should've been Winston that suffered not Elijah.

Elijah and Elsa are back from their little outing. She's helping him to his chair. He walks with difficulty these days. He's all stooped over and moves very slow. Elsa is so gentle with him.

"Thank you Elsa, for such a wonderful day."

"You're welcome, but it was no problem. It was such a beautiful day. I enjoyed it immensely. Is there anything I can get you?"

"A cup of coffee would be nice."

"Okay, I'll go brew some up now."

"Thank you."

When Elsa goes to the kitchen she starts crying. She seems quite upset. Her hands are shaking. I wonder what is wrong. She's such a good woman, even in her distress she continues to make Elijah's coffee.

When she returns with his coffee, she sits down by his side.

"She takes Elijah's hand in hers and says "Elijah, I have something I must tell you. I was at the Taylor's house that day. I was in Mrs. Taylor's garden club. I asked her if I could use her bathroom.   When I entered the house I overheard Winston and Sarah fighting. I quietly walked over to the doorway and looked in just in time to see Winston push Sarah down the stairs."

"I can still hear Sarah's scream. It chills me to this very day. I was eight years old when it happened. I was so scared I ran straight home and told my parents. However they forbid me to tell anyone because the Cargills had a lot of power in town.

When you started telling me this story I knew who you were talking about. I never said anything because my husband Sam is very good friends with Winston. So up until now I've been too afraid to say anything. However I'm going to the police station tomorrow and tell the truth about what happened that day. I may be a little late for work tomorrow."

Tears began falling down Elijah's face. He hugs Elsa real tight and says. "Thank you so much."

The next morning Elijah is awakened by the sound of police sirens. He can tell they are on Main Street heading downtown toward the courthouse. He begins to smile as he lies back on his pillow. For the first time in a long time I can tell he feels at peace. After all these years, justice is finally being served.

THE END

STORY TWO

ALEX

Alex's house

There is a wedding being held on my premises today. The groom has spared no expense. Each table is graced with white linen tablecloths and a bouquet of red roses. Red plush carpet was placed down the aisle leading to an archway covered in red and white roses. The five tier wedding cake perched over a water fountain is quite impressive as well.

The groom and groomsmen are decked out in black tuxes, starched white shirts and red cummerbunds. The bridesmaids are quite striking in their red silk dresses.

The musicians are all set up and ready to go. The wedding is supposed to start in about an hour. However the bride hasn't shown up yet. The groom looks very worried. Some of the guests are whispering amongst themselves. Word has it that the groom is about to get stood up at the altar.

Oh, I hope that is not the case. He needs her so badly. He didn't think he needed anyone at first. In fact when he first met her, he didn't even give her a second look. Then came the day he saw her in a different light. She wasn't very impressed by his newfound interest, but intrigued nonetheless. I bet you're wondering what I mean by that.

So let's venture back in time to the beginning of my story.

I was built in a prestigious neighborhood in sunny California. My lawn was beautifully landscaped. I was well built and not a shingle out of place. You would think I would've been happy.

Not!

You see the man that lived within my walls was very self involved. His only ambition in life was to be rich and famous. He was very wealthy and he wanted everyone to know it. I was one of the many possessions that he liked to flaunt. His only redeeming quality was that he could sing. He has a deep raspy voice. I enjoy listening to him immensely. I often thought, too bad he can't sing all the time. His name is Alexander Savant. However no one dared to call him that. He wanted to be called Alex. He said it sounded more masculine.

It really chapped my siding how he treated those who worked for him. The woman that cleaned me did a superb job. I always smelled really good after she came. She would pick flowers from my garden and display them on the kitchen table. However, he never thanked her. The only time she heard from him was when he needed her to do something extra. She would just smile and take it all in stride.

Her name is Emmy Montgomery. Although she was young, she seemed wise for her years. She took pride in her work. She was diligent and thorough. I always looked forward to the days she worked. I enjoyed the music she listened to. When she was on break she would call her best friend, or at least I think it was her best friend. Nonetheless she was talking to her friend.

I enjoyed hearing a conversation with some substance. You see I didn't hear that very often. Unless you think that breast augmentation, Botox, or somebody's new car is substance. Let's just say, the time with her was refreshing.

I learned a lot about Emmy by listening to those conversations. Cleaning houses wasn't her life ambition. However you would've thought so by how well she did her job. Emmy took care of me like I was her own. She was working days and taking college courses at night to become a counselor. You see, Emmy really wanted to make a difference in people's lives.

I always thought that Alex could use some counseling. Although he seemed to have his life together, and certainly portrayed much confidence, I wondered if he wasn't hiding behind the façade of fame and fortune. Quite often he had nightmares and would wake up in the middle of the night in a cold sweat.

I knew then that something in his past was haunting him.However in the light of day you would've thought he was on top of the world. He already had three number one songs. Several recording companies wanted him on their label. His stardom had quickly risen. Unfortunately it had gone to his head. He had cut ties with all his former friends. In fact he had very little to do with anyone that wasn't instrumental in furthering his career. This included those who worked for him.

The day Emmy came to apply for the job he didn't even bother to do the interview. He had his manager do it. After she had been working there for a while, Alex would occasionally peak his head in the door and tell her something he wanted added to the list of chores for that day. Other than that there was little contact between the two of them.

I always thought Emmy was more beautiful than any of the girls Alex had dated. She had a grace about her that none of them could match.

However, Alex was too blind to see it. His preference was tall skinny blondes. He liked them well endowed and all glamed up. After observing some of these women, it became quite clear to me why blonde jokes were so popular. I have to admit that being Alex's home was sometimes quite entertaining.

One day I overheard Emmy and her friend talking about an encounter she had with Alex. I found this to be quite comical.

Emmy had just completed her midterms and had passed with flying colors. She wanted to celebrate. The last few months had been especially hard so she decided to treat herself. She and a few friends got all dressed up and had a girl's night out.

Although it was quite pricey she chose the Ranada club. That place had it all, atmosphere, great food, and dancing. They arrived there about 7 o'clock. The place was packed. However she had made reservations earlier that week.

Unbeknownst to her Alex was there that night. What happened next makes me laugh to this day. It's a good thing we live in California, because when I laugh my windows rattle. Alex just thinks it's a small tremor.

Once they were settled, Emmy ordered a bottle of wine. They were all laughing and having a good time when Alex approached their table.

"Hello beautiful, you want to dance?"

When Emmy saw who it was she turned to her friend thinking he must be talking to her.

Alex put his hand on Emmy's shoulder and said, "I was talking to you beautiful."

Emmy turned back toward Alex with a perplexed look.

"Are you kidding me, don't you know who I am?"

"Should I?"

"Yeah, I believe so."

"Well let's dance and you can fill me in."

Emmy turned to her friends and winked. Then she and Alex went out on the dance floor.

"Are you sure we've met? I think I would've remembered you. What's your name?"

"Oh no, you are not getting off that easy."

Alex twirled her around and said "Okay, so where do you work?"

"I have my own business."

"What kind of business?"

"Let's just say I provide a service for the community."

"Have you provided me this service?"

"As a matter of fact I have."

"Was I pleased?"

"I'm not sure. You say very little to me when I'm at your house."

Emmy said at this point, Alex looked shocked and said, "Emmy?"

"Yes."

"Wow, you clean up well!"

"Being punny, are we?"

"No, I didn't even think of that. I just meant you dress up nice."

"How would you know? I've been working for you over a year and I don't believe you've ever looked me in the face."

"What can I say, I'm a busy man."

"Well that may be so, but I have always thought you were just stuck up."

"Ouch! I'm talking to you now."

"Yeah, because you thought I was someone else."

"Okay, you got me there. Would it help if I told you how pleased I am with your work?"

"Maybe."

"Emmy, I don't know what I'd do without you."

By this time Emmy was smiling and said " Now was that so difficult?"

Alex just smiled.

"Okay all kidding aside, that was very nice of you to say. However I did come with friends and I really need to get back to them."

"Maybe we can get together sometime."

"Maybe"

After hearing that bit of information, I thought to myself, 'Wow Alex was actually nice. Maybe there's hope for him after all.'

I bet Emmy looked stunning that night. She has such striking features. She's a brunette and has long cascading curls. Her eyes are a deep brown. It's no wonder Alex took notice. Although it took him long enough.

Emmy did say she thought Alex was handsome. She mentioned liking his tall stature, broad shoulders, and piercing blue eyes. Then she quickly added "but I doubt that it goes anywhere."

Then I heard Alex's side of the story. He told his manager that he had met a hot girl at the Ranada club. Then he went on and on about how pretty she was and how he had to see her again. It was funny though, he never mentioned it was Emmy. I thought that was odd because he and his manager were really close friends.

Later that evening, I overheard him talking on the phone to Emmy. He asked her if she would like to come over for dinner Friday night. He told her he grilled a mean steak. I knew she had accepted his invitation because when he got off the phone he stood in front of the mirror, flexed his biceps and said 'you've still got it, Alex.'

That was one of those times Alex thought he felt a small tremor.

That Friday Alex seemed a little nervous. He had tried on several outfits before settling on dark jeans and a white shirt. After he showered and shaved, he put on his favorite cologne. Then he stood there and critiqued himself in front of the mirror for what seemed forever.

I don't believe I had ever seen Alex that concerned about his looks.

Then I remembered that his father had called him earlier that day. Alex told him about his date with Emmy. He mentioned how pretty she was, and that although she was a little younger than him, she had agreed to go out with him. I'm not sure what his dad said, but Alex seemed really down after that.

Alex's mother had died when he was real young. It was just he and his father for many years. When he was fifteen, his father remarried. Instantly he had a stepmom and two stepsisters. All he ever said about that time of his life was that he was pretty much on his own. Alex rarely saw his dad and when he did he seemed very uncomfortable. He didn't have any pictures of his family displayed, nor did he talk much about his childhood. I always wondered if that had something to do with his nightmares.

Once Alex was dressed he went downstairs and started up the grill. The steaks had been marinating all day. He had come up with his own special marinade. Then he put his favorite champagne on ice and took out some crystal stemware. Alex was known for being a great host. I could tell he was very pleased with how everything was coming together.

Emmy showed up right on time. She wore a white peasant blouse and capris. Her hair was up in a French twist. She looked lovely. I could tell that Alex thought so too.

She brought a homemade cheesecake for dessert.

Alex graciously thanked her.

After setting down the cheesecake, she looked around the room and said "Wow you have a very nice home. You must have a great housekeeper. Your house is immaculate."

Alex laughed and said "Yeah, she's a keeper."

"Would you like some champagne?"

"Yes, thank you."

"The steaks are on the grill and I made baked potatoes and a salad. I thought we might eat out on the patio, if that's okay with you."

"Sounds good to me. It's a beautiful evening."

Alex motioned for her to follow him. Emmy was quite surprised when she stepped out on the patio.

The table was set, complete with tablecloth, linen napkins, two place settings, and a single lit candle in the center of the table. There was soft music playing in the background.

"Wow you sure went all out. You're quite the host, Alex."

"Well when you told me the other night that you have worked for me over a year, I thought we would celebrate."

"I still can't believe you didn't know who I was."

"Let's not go there for fear that it might incriminate me. Let's just start with a clean slate."

Emmy laughed and said, "Okay, clean slate it is."

Emmy sat down at the table while Alex checked on the steaks. She looked around at all of the beautiful shrubbery and flowers and said, "It's so pretty here. Don't you think Tom does such a good job?"

"Who's Tom?"

"Your gardener"

"Oh, I didn't know his name."

"Maybe you should take the time to get to know him, not only is he a phenomenal gardener but he's a very nice man as well."

"Point taken, The steaks aren't quite done, so why don't you tell me a little bit about yourself."

"Well, my name is Emmy Montgomery and I am 29 years old."

At that point Alex looked a little surprised. Emmy noticed and asked if something was wrong.

"Well I just realized I'm 11 years older than you."

"Is that a problem for you?"

"Not if it isn't for you. Please continue."

"Well as you know, I clean houses for a living. However that's not what I want to do for the rest of my life. I'm studying to be a counselor. I have one more semester and I'll graduate."

"What made you choose that career?"

"There are so many people who have suffered some sort of abuse and are really messed up. I really want to help them deal with their pain."

"That's very kind of you, Emmy. Do you have any siblings?"

"Yes, one brother and one sister."

"Do your parents live close?"

"My mother does. My father died of cancer a couple of years ago."

"Oh I'm so sorry."

"Thanks, I'm just glad he's not suffering any more. Do you have any brothers or sisters, Alex?"

"No. My father has a couple of stepdaughters, but we never were close."

"Oh did your parents divorce?"

"No, my mother died when I was really young."

"Sounds like we both had tragedies."

It became very obvious to Emmy that Alex wasn't comfortable talking about his family so she quickly changed the subject.

"So what made you decide to become a singer?"

"Well, I've always loved music. You might say it was my Savior when I was younger. When I was 15 I got my first guitar and I have been playing every since. However I didn't get my first break till I was 30. I was playing in a local club and a big record producer just happened to be there that night. He came up and introduced himself. I about fell off my chair when I found out he was Charles Donovan. This man had helped countless artists launch their careers. He told me that I was very talented and would like to help me with my career."

"That was a lucky break."

"Yeah, I was pretty psyched! Oh, I better check on the steaks."

Alex and Emmy seemed to really have a good time that night. There was alot of laughing and cutting up. It's no wonder though, Emmy is quite comical.

When Emmy got ready to leave, Alex walked her to the car. When she turned around after unlocking the door, there was Alex staring down at her. He pulled her close and gently kissed her. Although he didn't ask, Emmy didn't seem to mind at all.

As the months passed they continued to see each other on a regular basis. However, I thought it was kind of strange that Alex never took Emmy to any of his regular hangouts.

Then one day it became quite clear why. Emmy came to clean me. When she came in, Alex was talking to his manager and a couple of record producers.

She went over to Alex and said, "Hi," expecting to be introduced to his guests.

Alex said in a matter of fact way "Oh, I'm so glad you're here Ms. Montgomery. Your list of chores is in the kitchen. I'll be in to discuss it with you shortly."

Emmy was taken back by his curt response. Nonetheless she headed for the kitchen, but before leaving the room she turned to him and said,"By the way Mr. Savant your girlfriend called, she said not to bother calling her again because she doesn't want to go out with you anymore."

Alex looked very shocked. He told his manager that he had something to take care of and quickly headed to the kitchen.

"What do you mean you don't want to go out with me anymore?"

"I think what I said was quite clear."

"But, why?"

"I think I'm the one that should be asking that question. Why in the world did you treat me so coldly in front of your friends?"

"I haven't told anybody about us yet."

"Why? Are you ashamed of me?'

"No, it's just that I'm not sure how people will respond to the idea of me dating my housekeeper."

It was at that point that I about fell off my foundation. I couldn't believe he said that. So what happened next didn't surprise me at all.

"Oh don't worry about that because as of right now you are not dating your housekeeper. I deserve being with someone who is proud to be with me and would shout it from the rooftops."

"I know, you do deserve better than that. I'm so sorry, but I'm just not ready to reveal our relationship."

"Then I guess it's over for us Alex, because I can't be with someone who considers me a possible embarrassment. However I won't leave you in a bind. I'll continue to work here till you can find someone to replace me."

"I don't want you to quit. Nobody can replace you."

"I just think it would be best if we separate completely."

After saying that, Emmy walked out of the room. I could tell Alex was very upset, but he didn't go after her. It was good that Emmy stood up for herself but I sure was disappointed with the outcome. Alex really needed her. He was just too hardheaded to admit it.

Later that evening after Emmy had finished cleaning, she came into the living room to see if Alex needed her to do anything else before she headed home.

Without looking up he said, "No, but thanks for asking."

Emmy lingered in the doorway as though she wanted to say something but then turned around to leave. Stopping once again she turned to him and said "for what it's worth Alex, it was nice while it lasted."

At that he looked up, smiled and said "Yeah, it was."

She smiled back and headed out the door.

Oh, how I wanted Alex to rush after her, but he didn't.

Several weeks passed and Alex hadn't even tried to find a new housekeeper.

When Emmy asked him about it he said, "I'm having a hard time finding someone. Could you give me just a few more weeks?"

Emmy, being the kind person she is, agreed to stay.

On several occasions when Emmy wasn't working, Alex would find any excuse to call her. For instance "Do you know where the long handled spatula is?" *or* "I can't find my white shirt."

Alex wasn't fooling anyone. It was quite clear that he was missing Emmy. I think Emmy missed him too because she never seem to be bothered by his calls. However neither one of them was going to give in first. They were both very stubborn.

Sometimes when Emmy came to clean me, I would catch Alex staring at her while she worked. It was obvious to me that he was in love with her. Sometimes I just wanted to drop one of my light fixtures on his hard head.

When Alex found out he was going on tour, he asked her if she would work for him a little while longer. His excuse was that he didn't want a stranger in his house while he was gone. Once again Emmy agreed. I don't think Emmy was ready to let go either. That made me really happy because I would've missed her immensely.

The day Alex was to leave on tour, he was in a panic because he hadn't finished packing and couldn't find his suitcases. So he called Emmy to come and help him. She found his suitcases out in the garage on the top shelf. I thought that was funny because that's where Alex always kept them. They were pretty dusty so she cleaned them up. When she went into his room to help him pack she noticed a picture of a young woman on his nightstand. The picture was old and worn.

"Who's this Alex?"

"That's my mother's sister, Stella. She was my favorite aunt."

"Do you see her often?"

"No, I haven't seen her since I was 10."

"Why is that?"

"She and my dad had a fight. So he moved us far away and I never saw her again. I loved her very much. She always made me feel so special. I think of her often."

"Have you ever thought about getting in touch with her?"

"No I haven't. It would be great to see her, but I wouldn't even know how to go about getting in touch with her. I don't even know what her last name would be now. However I've never forgotten how good she was to me. She was there for me after my mother's death."

"Sounds like she was a special lady"

"She was."

Alex turned away from Emmy. I could see tears in his eyes. He didn't want her to see him cry so he headed to the bathroom. His excuse was that he needed to get his shaving kit. She knew better, but didn't let on.

When he came out of the bathroom she was closing up his suitcases.

"You're all packed up."

"Thank you so much. I really don't know what I would do without you. I sure wish you'd reconsider and keep working for me."

Emmy wiped one lingering tear from his cheek and said "We will talk about that when you get back. Now you better go so you don't miss your plane."

"Okay, thanks again." *Without even thinking Alex hugged her tightly and kissed her on the cheek.*

She just smiled and said, "Get on out of here."

I remember thinking that those two belong together.

While Alex was on tour, Emmy came over regularly to water the plants, bring in the mail, and do a few extras that she hadn't had time to do in her regular rounds. One day while she was there the doorbell rang. When she opened the door, there stood a tall older gentleman with a suitcase in tow.

Emmy just smiled and said "May I help you?"

"Well, yes, you can. Grab this suitcase and take it in while I go get the rest of my things."

"Excuse me?"

"I think I was quite clear."

"May I ask who you are?"

"The name is John savant. I'm Alex's father. Is he at home?"

"I'm so sorry but he's on tour right now. Did he not tell you that?"

"We hadn't talked lately. I intended to surprise him."

Emmy picked up the suitcase and said "Please come in."

"Thank you."

"I'm sure Alex wouldn't mind if you stay here tonight."

"I just might have to take you up on that. I don't know when I can get a flight back home."

"Would you like help getting the rest of your things?"

"No, it's just one more suitcase. I'll get it later."

"Please sit down and make yourself at home. Mr. Savant. Could I get you something to drink?"

"Do you have any beer?"

"I don't think so. Alex isn't much of a beer drinker."

"Oh yeah, I forgot, that boy's always been such a pansy."

"Is there something else I can get you?"

"No, that's okay. I'll just go out and get something later. So who are you?"

"I am Emmy, Alex's housekeeper. I'm taking care of the place while he is away."

"He has a housekeeper?"

"Yes Sir."

"Well, if he would be a man and get a real job, he might could find himself a wife."

"He's got a real job. He is a professional singer and has done quite well for himself."

"Yeah, whatever, from the looks of things he's probably in a lot of debt."

I could tell Emmy was shocked by his unkind remarks. However that was just the beginning. The whole time he was here he had nothing good to say about Alex.

Even when he talked to him on the phone he was very negative and critical.

It became quite clear to Emmy and me why Alex was so self-conscious and worried about how others viewed him. For so long I couldn't stand Alex, but at that time I actually felt sorry for him.

Emmy told her friend that being around John was depressing and she was glad he was gone. It was funny though how she described him. She said he looked like an older version of Alex until he opened his mouth. That was one time that Emmy felt a small tremor.

Several days passed without a single soul dropping by. It was very quiet around here. I have to admit that I was a little lonely. However there were some people who stopped and took pictures of me. It was apparent that Alex was becoming even more popular. I thought to myself 'too bad Alex's father couldn't see it.' I wondered if he had ever heard Alex sing. Because after hearing him sing you can't help but want to hear more. Every day there were messages from managers wanting him to sing at their upcoming events. I was so happy for him.

The day Alex was coming home, Emmy was here bright and early. My windows were opened to air me out.

Since there weren't any fresh flowers in the garden that time of year, Emmy bought some from the florist. They were beautiful. She put fresh clean sheets on his bed and then began to inspect each of my rooms to make sure they were clean.

I don't think I ever saw her move so fast. I got the impression she didn't want to be here when Alex got home. However he showed up earlier than expected. She was down on her knees cleaning under the coffee table when she heard him come through the door.

"I'm home."

When she looked up her hair fell down on her face. She quickly brushed it back and saw Alex smiling down at her. Then she said "Well, hello stranger."

Alex just smiled and helped her up. He pulled her close and said, "I sure have missed you."

"Yeah right, I bet you had girls all over you."

"I won't say they didn't try, but I only have eyes for you."

"So you think you can just come in here and act like we never broke up?"

"That's what I was hoping." *Then he pulled her even closer and tenderly kissed her.*

I guess Emmy didn't mind because she didn't try to stop him. After that, Alex showed Emmy a newscast on the Internet. It was one of his interviews while on tour. He was asked if he was dating anyone. Alex said, "Yes, her name is Emmy Montgomery and I am crazy about her." *When asked how they met he said,* "She is my housekeeper."

Emmy was moved to tears and she hugged him and said "Oh Alex I'm crazy about you too."

I saw a softer side of Alex that day and I must admit the man was growing on me. I was really glad they were back together because, like I said before, Alex really needed Emmy. Her being back in his life could not have come at a better time.

When Alex returned from touring, I noticed that his nightmares were increasing as well as intensifying. Sometimes he wouldn't fall asleep until the wee hours of the morning. One morning when Emmy came to clean me, Alex wasn't up yet.

*She was cleaning the kitchen when she heard Alex
screaming. She ran to his room and found him
thrashing around as though fighting off someone.
She quickly tried to wake him up. By that time Alex
was in tears.* She held him tenderly in her arms and
whispered, "It's okay, Alex. I'm here for you."

*Alex let out a lot of pent up emotions that morning.
It was the first time I ever heard him talk about his
childhood. Emmy just sat quietly and listened.*

"When I was six years old my mother was killed in a
car wreck. My father was overcome with grief. At
one point it was so bad that he had to be
hospitalized for quite some time. I stayed with my
Aunt Stella. She was so good to me. I remember
her getting down on the floor and playing with me.
Then each night she would read me a story and say
a prayer with me. After my mother died that was
the only place I ever felt secure.

"When my dad got out of the hospital, he became a
recluse in his own home. My mother's family did
what they could to help him. However it was well
over a year before he went back to work. Although
my aunt didn't think it was a good idea, my dad
insisted I come home. That was when my world
became a living hell.

"My dad's way of dealing with his loss was whiskey, and a lot of it. One night when he was real drunk he came into my room. He told me to go do the dishes. I asked him if I could finish my homework first. He hit me so hard that I fell off the bed. He jerked me up and said 'don't talk back to me boy. Get in there and do the dishes.'

"I hurried to the kitchen and he followed. He commenced telling me that I was worthless and that it was all my fault that my mother had died.

"'You just had to have ice cream that night, didn't you boy? You're nothing but a selfish little brat."

"When I started crying he came over and hit me again and told me if I didn't quit crying he would give me something to cry about. That was the last time I ever cried in front of my dad."

It was at this point that Emmy put her arm around Alex and said "Do you feel responsible for your mother's death?"

"I did at first, but my Aunt Stella told me on more than one occasion that it was a horrible accident and it wasn't my fault."

"Did you believe her?"

"I do now."

"When I told my aunt what happened that night, she told my dad that if it happened again she would call the authorities."

"Did he stop?"

"For a little while but it wasn't long and he was back at it again. It started out just verbal abuse then it escalated to physical abuse. He knocked me out on more than one occasion."

"Oh my goodness, Alex, that's horrible."

"He told me I better not say anything, because they would send him to jail and he would have to kill himself. Then he would say 'you wouldn't want to be responsible for both your parent's deaths, would you?'"

"Oh Alex, I'm so sorry. No child should have to endure that."

"It wasn't until I was 10 that my aunt noticed a bruise on my leg. When she asked me about it, I told her I had fallen. I don't think she believed me because she confronted my dad later that night. That's when they had the big fight that led him to move us far away. At first he made it an adventure. He promised me he was going to quit drinking and make a better life for the two of us. He told me he loved me and that nobody was going to take me away from him. It was great for a while."

"Then he started drinking again. So it wasn't long until he was abusing me again."

"When did he finally stop?"

"When I was 15 he met Susan. So he sobered up and put on a show for her and her daughters. It wasn't long into the relationship that they got married. One time when I was 17, he and Susan had come back from a party and he was pretty lit. He tried bullying me and I stood up to him. He never messed with me again. It wasn't long after that I left home."

"Is this the first time you've talked to someone about this?"

"Yes."

"You know, Alex, it might do you some good to see a therapist."

"Oh, I don't know about that, but I'll think about it."

"Well, whatever you decide, I'll be here for you."

Alex caressed her cheek and said, "Thanks, I appreciate that."

"You must be starving. Let me go and fix you something to eat."

When Emmy got up to head to the kitchen, Alex pulled her back down and passionately kissed her and said, "I love you so much."

Emmy gently pressed her forehead against his and said, "I love you too."

From that moment on, those two were inseparable. Although both of them were really busy, they always managed to find time for each other. Sometimes Emmy would watch Alex rehearse. Then he would help her study. All that mattered to them was that they were together.

Alex did decide to go to therapy. I could tell it was helping because his nightmares decreased tremendously.

One evening while cuddling on the couch and watching a movie, the phone rang. It was Alex's manager. He told him that he was nominated for male vocalist of the year.

Alex was so excited that he picked Emmy up and swirled her around and around.

Laughing she said, "What are you so excited about?"

"I've been nominated for male vocalist of the year!"

Squealing with delight Emmy exclaimed , "Oh, I'm so happy for you Alex!"

"I've been wanting this for a long time."

"You deserve it Alex, you are an awesome vocalist ."

"Thanks, but you might be a little biased."

"Maybe so, but you're awesome nonetheless. So when is the awards ceremony?"

"The ceremony is only six weeks away. So we have a lot to do. We need to find something to wear and I need to prepare an acceptance speech in case I win. Then we need to plan a party for afterwards."

"Don't worry, we will get it all done. It's going to be a magical night."

Things were going real well for Alex until he began to receive multiple calls from his father. He asked if he could come and visit a few days. Apparently he wanted to mend their severed relationship.

That very night Alex had a bad nightmare. After that he couldn't go back to sleep. When the sun came up the next morning he was still wide awake. I could tell he was in a quandary as to whether he should talk to his father, or put it off for a little longer.

Emmy came over that evening to fix dinner for the two of them. She was setting the table when he came back from therapy. She could tell something was wrong because he came into the room without saying a thing and sat down at the table.

"Alex , is something wrong?"

"I haven't told you yet, but my father has been calling. He wants to come for a visit. Apparently he wants us to have a relationship. He abused me as a child, basically abandoned me at 15 and now he wants to have a relationship."

"Frankly, Emmy, I don't know if I even want a relationship with the man. So I went to my therapist to ask him what I should do. I got nothing."

"He can't tell you what to do, Alex. He can only help you explore your options."

"I already know my options. I just don't know what to do."

"You must have some idea of what you want to do."

"Yeah, avoid the situation altogether, but that won't solve anything."

"So what do you think will solve the problem?"

"You sound just like my therapist."

"You think?"

They both had to laugh.

"I know I have to confront my father in order to let go of my past, but as far as having a relationship with him, I just don't know.   None of this is going to be easy."

"I'm here for you Alex."

Alex kissed her hand and said, "I am so glad you're in my life."

Emmy had made Alex's favorite meal. Lasagna, salad, and bread sticks. Then she poured him a glass of wine and they sat down for a leisurely dinner.

The day John was to arrive, Alex was a nervous wreck. When Emmy showed up, she found him pacing the floor.

She hugged him and said "Everything will be all right."

He held on to her for quite some time. I could see his body trembling. Emmy tried her best to calm him.

About that time the doorbell rang. Emmy went to answer it, while Alex composed himself. When she opened the door, there stood John.

"Well hello there, it's nice to see you again."

"It's nice to see you, Mr. Savant. Please come in."

When he saw Alex he immediately went over to hug him.

Although Alex allowed it, I could see his body stiffen as his dad hugged him.

"It's good to see you, son. I appreciate you letting me come to visit."

"No problem. Please sit down and make yourself comfortable."

"Would you mind if I lie down for a while? I am really tired from my trip."

Alex showed him to his room. Then he and Emmy went to the kitchen to prepare dinner.

Later that evening, after dinner, Alex and his father adjourned to the living room.

John was looking around the room and said, "You have a nice place here."

"Thanks, I'm quite proud of it."

"Well, just be careful that you don't get in to a lot of debt."

"I'm not in debt, I'm doing quite well with my singing career. In fact, I've been nominated for male vocalist of the year."

"So you're telling me that you're singing got you all this?"

"Yes."

"Well, if you're so rich and famous, why aren't you married yet?   I was under the impression that male singers always have a lot of women after them."

"There was a time I did.   However I'm with Emmy now, and she is my one and only."

"Your housekeeper?"

"Yes, you have a problem with that?"

"You sure she isn't after your money?"

"You better be really careful what you say next, because you're talking about the woman I love."

"SORRY!"

"Dad, why did you come here? I mean we haven't had a relationship in years. Why does it matter to you now?"

"You're my son, and I would like us to be close again."

"And how do you propose we do that?"

"Well you know, getting together and talking like we're doing now."

"We've been sitting here for five minutes and you have already accused me of being in debt, downplayed my career choice, and put my girlfriend down because she's a housekeeper. Then you had the gall to say she was after my money. I don't think we're off to good start, Dad."

"Okay, let's try again. So how did your last tour go?"

"I think there's something else that we need to talk about first."

"And that would be?"

"How about my childhood?   I think you own me an apology."

"For what?"

"Oh, I don't know, Dad, maybe for the fact that you abused me my whole childhood. That you blamed me for my mother's death.   And let's not forget that you took me away from my aunt Stella, only to abandon me when you married Susan."

"Do we have to bring up the past? I was a broken man back then."

"Oh I'm sorry Dad, I should have been stronger. After all, I was seven years old."

"I know your life wasn't easy, but I can't go back and change that."

"No, you can't, but you can admit that you were a drunk and an abuser, and say you're sorry.   And you could certainly be less critical of me now and treat me with respect."

"Well, you're not being very respectful to me. And I don't have to take this."

"No, Dad you don't, but when I was a little boy I had no choice but to take it. However, I'm not a little boy anymore, so unless you can say you're sorry, and attempt to treat me with the respect I deserve, we will never have a relationship."

It was at this point that John got up and walked out. He went into his room and slammed the door.

Emmy came out of the kitchen to see what all the commotion was. Alex was sitting on the couch alone.

"Where's your dad, Alex?"

"He got upset when I confronted him, so he went to his room and slammed the door."

Emmy put her arm around Alex and said, "I'm so sorry."

"Me too."

The next morning when Alex got up, his dad was long gone.

The awards ceremony was quickly approaching. So Emmy started making plans for the big party afterwards. To keep his mind busy she got Alex involved in preparing for the festivities.

However, unbeknownst to her, Alex was planning his own big surprise. He wanted to re-create the night of their first date, but on this date, he would get down on one knee and propose. The ring he bought was breathtaking. He asked her to come over for dinner because he wanted to discuss an idea he had for the party.

When she arrived he directed her into the kitchen. There on the bar was a bottle of Dom Perignon.

"Would you like some champagne?"

"Sure."

"Let's sit on the patio while we wait on the steaks"

When Emmy stepped out on the patio she was quite surprised. The table was set for two with a single lit candle in the middle,and there was music playing in the background.

"Wow, Alex, you went all out!" *Putting her arms around his neck she said,* "you don't have to impress me anymore."

"Oh, I just wanted to make you dinner because I haven't done it in a while. Please sit down while I go check on dinner."

"Let me help you."

"No, I've got it."

When he returned he had only one thing in his hand. A small, little black box. He walked over to Emmy and got down on one knee and said, "I used to look at women for how pretty they were and how good they make me look, and although you are very beautiful, that's not what I see when I look at you. I see the woman I love and want to spend the rest of my life with. So Emmy Montgomery, would you please be my wife?"

Huge tears welled up in Emmy's eyes as she looked down at Alex and said, "Yes, Alex, I would be honored to be your wife."

Alex stood up and placed the ring on her finger. Then he pulled her close to him and passionately kissed her. I don't think I ever saw them happier than at that very moment. They spent the rest of the evening talking about their future.

The day of the awards ceremony finally arrived I was all decorated for the party afterward. Alex had hired a caterer so my kitchen was full of people preparing for the guests that would arrive later that evening. Emmy had just returned from the salon. She looked beautiful. She and Alex hurriedly dressed and were whisked away in a limousine.

Later that evening my walls were buzzing with activity. It was quite evident that Alex had won the award for male vocalist of the year. His award was already displayed on my mantle. However that wasn't the top subject of the night. It seems that when Alex gave his acceptance speech he had Emmy stand up and he told the audience as well as all the people watching on TV that she was his fiancée and that they plan to marry in the spring.

There were mixed feelings among the guests. Some thought it was sweet, others a bit over-the-top.

One of Alex's ex-girlfriends had a little too much to drink and was quite vocal that she wasn't happy about Alex's upcoming nuptials. She was one of those blondes he had dated in the past. However a book of blonde jokes could've been written on her alone. Her name was Barbie, need I say more?

I was a complete mess after that party was over. Emmy showed up bright and early the next morning to clean me. Alex stopped her and said he had hired a crew to come in and clean up because he didn't want her to have to do it. Then he said, "But I think it's sweet that you wanted to."

I bet you're dying to know if Emmy ever showed up at her own wedding. Well at this moment there is not a soul inside my walls. It's dark and quiet, but let me tell you about what went on earlier under my roof. It was about 15 minutes till the wedding was supposed to start. The wedding planner had seated all the guests and the band was entertaining them.

Alex was looking longingly out the front window. He had tried calling Emmy several times to no avail. His manager received a call, and came in and told Alex that he was needed in the kitchen.

"For what?"

"I don't know, but it sounded important."

Alex headed to the kitchen and then I saw why he was being steered away from the window. Emmy was coming up the sidewalk with her wedding dress in tow. There was an older woman with her. I wondered who she was.

I thought it was odd but she rang the doorbell. Alex came running from the kitchen to answer the door. When he opened the door he couldn't believe his eyes, standing there before him was his Aunt Stella. He reached out to hug her. It was very touching because that was the first time he had hugged her in 30 years.

He then kissed her forhead and said, "It's so good to see you, Aunt Stella."

She patted him on his cheeks and said, 'it's good to see you too Alexander. You have turned into quite a handsome man."

Alex turned to Emmy and said, "How in the world did you find her?"

Emmy just smiled and said, "I have my ways."

"Thank you so much."

Emmy is hurried up the stairs to get dressed so that the wedding could proceed. Aunt Stella is seated in front with the rest of the family while Alex goes to the front to await his bride.

When Emmy enters the room the band begins to play. Her brother walks her down the aisle.

Alex and Emmy's eyes are intent on each other. It's such a beautiful scene.

Her brother places her hand in Alex's and sits down. Just as the minister is about to start, one last guest enters the room. It's Alex's father.

He looked at his son and smiled then putting his hand to his heart he mouthed, "I'm so sorry."

Alex smiles and nods his head in acknowledgment.

Once they said their vows and exchanged rings, the minister said, "I now pronounce you husband and wife. You may kiss the bride."

 111

Alex pulled back Emmy's veil and said , "Hello beautiful."   Then he gently kissed her.

THE END

.

STORY THREE

AMELIA

Amelia's house

For so long I've been afraid of facing a home's worst fear. That of being abandoned. You see I've been vacant for quite some time now. My Windows are locked and the shades are pulled. It's so dark and quiet within my walls. Oh, how I long to feel the sun shine through my Windows.

The grandfather clock that once kept me company by chiming every hour on the hour has long been silent. The white sheets used to protect my furniture are all dingy and tattered by mice seeking refuge from the cold winter nights.

It seems like an eternity since they came and took Mrs. Stanton away. She had fallen on several occasions. So her daughter Grace thought it was best that she go live with her.

Since then, no one has lived within these walls, unless you count the homeless that from time to time take shelter under my roof. I have to admit I was thankful for the company as well as the little bit of sunshine that peaked through my window they had broken.

However, I think things are about to change.

Just this morning a couple came in and toured my many rooms. The gentleman took numerous notes of repairs that I need. Although the woman never said a word, she looked very familiar to me. It wasn't until he began to communicate with her through sign language that I realized who she might be. Then I thought to myself, could this really be her? I bet you're wondering who I'm talking about.

So let's venture back in time to the beginning of my story.

It was 1924 and America was in the midst of what we now call the roaring 20s. It was a time of hope and economic prosperity.

I was built in Dearborn Michigan for Joseph and Clara Stanton. I wasn't your typical bungalow common for that area. Clara Stanton would have nothing less than a three-story Victorian home complete with a large porch and columns.

Joseph had been recently hired by the Ford Motor Company to oversee the production line of the model T Ford. Clara had inherited quite a bit of money when her father died. So when it came to me, they spared no expense. I had a lot of amenities that few houses had at that time. This included electricity.

Prior to move-in day, I had only seen Mr. Stanton
twice. However Mrs. Stanton was here quite
regularly. She had plenty to say about how things
were progressing, or lack thereof. What she
wanted seemed to change from day to day.
I could tell that the contractor was very frustrated.

I was a little bit confused about the design of my top
floor. It was to have its own private staircase and
could only be accessed from my second floor. It
consisted of only three rooms. Two small bedrooms
and one full bath. There was one window in each
bedroom and they were quite elevated and
relatively small. So they weren't very useful to say
the least. It was obvious that Mrs. Stanton had
very little interest in the decor of those rooms
because in comparison to all my other rooms they
were very plain.

When moving day finally arrived, Mrs. Stanton was
here bright and early. She was busy contemplating
the placement of each piece of furniture. When the
movers arrived they began unloading the boxes. I
noticed on each box, in flawless penmanship I might
add, was a list of its contents as well as in which
room it needed to go.

Once the boxes were unloaded, they brought in the
furniture and placed each piece in its designated
area. Then she had them assemble all the beds.

It was quite clear that Mrs. Stanton took a perfectionist attitude toward everything she did.

I thought it was odd that Mr. Stanton didn't arrive until later that night after the sun had set. Mrs. Stanton didn't even have my porch light on for him. I had overheard earlier that the Stantons had only one child. Her name was Grace and she was 10 years old. So I was a bit confused about what I saw next.

Little Grace was the first to enter. She was all giggles and smiles. She ran to her mother and hugged her. Then Mr. Stanton came in carrying something bundled up in a blanket. To my surprise it was another little girl. She was obviously younger than Grace and had a very different demeanor. While Grace was bubbling with enthusiasm, she just stood there very quietly next to Mr. Stanton and never said a word.

Before I could even contemplate who she was, another person entered the room. This time it was a girl that looked to be in her late teens. Although she was young she had a furrowed brow as though she was carrying a heavy load.

At first I was confused but it didn't take long and the troubles of this family became painfully clear.

There's a saying that most families have a skeleton in their closet. The Stanton's skeleton was a whole little girl. Her name is Amelia and she was born deaf.

At that time in history it was considered a disgrace to have a handicapped child. They kept her hidden away so that no one would know she existed.

The conversation that ensued that evening saddens me to this day.

"Are you sure no one saw her?"

"No Clara. I covered her up before I got out of the car. Besides it's pitch black out there. Nobody could have seen anything."

"I don't know why you're so concerned, Aunt Clara. It's's not like she has a disease or something."

"Eileen, do not talk to your aunt that way."

"Why are you defending her? You don't agree with it either."

"Joseph, is that true?"

"I just think we need to stop worrying about what other people think and do what's best for Amelia."

"What's best for Amelia is that her father has a job. We have to think about our reputation in the community. If anybody was to find out about Amelia we could lose everything we've worked for. You know how judgmental people can be, Joseph. So as far as I'm concerned this conversation is over."

Then she turned her back to Mr. Stanton and in a much sweeter tone said "Grace, would you like to see your new room?"

"Yes, Mommy, I would love to. Can daddy and Amelia come too?"

"Daddy will come with us, but I believe Eileen will be taking Amelia to see her own bedroom."

At that point all five of them went upstairs. I will never forget the look on Amelia's face as she walked by Grace's room. Although the room was beautifully done in light lavender with white crown molding, that wasn't what she was transfixed on.

Tears welled up in her eyes as she watched her parents playfully interact with Grace.

Eileen picked her up and gave her a big hug. Then they went up to the third floor.

I could see the disdain on Eileen's face as they entered Amelia's modest room. It was obvious that her aunt hadn't taken any pains with the decor of the room. The walls were painted white and there wasn't any crown molding. The small room barely held it's meager furnishings: a bed, night stand, dresser and an old antique trunk that was placed at the foot of the bed.

She set Amelia down on the bed and wiped the tears from her face. After kissing her tenderly on the forehead she motioned for Amelia to wait. She opened the old trunk and pulled out a teddy bear. Amelia immediately began making grunting sounds while reaching out for it. When Eileen handed it to her she held it tight and began rocking back-and-forth. That was the first time I saw her smile.

After Amelia fell asleep, Eileen went into her own bedroom. The room was similar to Amelia's. She collapsed on her bed and wept profusely. Although I knew her heart went out to Amelia I couldn't help but wonder if some of the tears she shed were for herself.

My suspicion was confirmed by a conversation I
overheard between the Stanton's later that night.
Once Grace was tucked into bed the Stanton's
retired to their bedroom. Mr. Stanton was lying in
bed reading over the manual for his new job, while
Mrs. Stanton was sitting at her dressing table
combing out her long hair.

I came to appreciate that this was their nightly ritual.
It was their time to talk about everyday occurrences
as well as serious matters that needed to be
addressed. The look on Mrs. Stanton's face told me
that she had something serious to discuss.

"Joseph, do you think we did the right thing by
taking Eileen in?"

"Why would you ask that?" *Mr. Stanton asked*
incredulously.

"Well, she was very disrespectful this evening."

He removed his glasses and with an emotional
voice said, "Clara, think about all she's been
through. First, she lost her parents and was
uprooted from the only home she ever knew to
come and live with us. Now we've moved and she's
had to leave all her friends behind and start all over
again. I think she just needs some time to adjust.

Besides, do you think we could find someone to take care of Amelia as well as Eileen does?"

Mrs. Stanton continued to comb her hair and then reluctantly said, "Probably not."

It was obvious that Eileen's pain ran deep. This touched me to the very core of my foundation. At that point I could only hope that my tears would be mistaken for tomorrow's morning dew.

For the next few weeks Mrs. Stanton worked tirelessly to put me in order. In no time she had me looking like they had lived in me for years. It was interesting watching her decorate. After meticulously arranging something she would step back and observe. Then she would move one item and step back again, only to move it again to exactly where it was before.

However, the most entertainment came when she and Mr. Stanton were hanging the pictures. He would hold the picture up while Mrs. Stanton stood back to make sure he put it up exactly where she wanted.

I could see the frustration on his face when she would say, "Just a little to the right," or "Just a little to the left." Sometimes it was "Just a little higher," or "Just a little lower." I don't know how many times he said, "Goodness woman, make up your mind."

I must admit I had to laugh at his expense. Any humorous moments, I welcomed. It was a nice distraction from the sorrow I normally felt for this family that lived under my roof.

However, watching Eileen and Amelia brought me great joy. The way she cared for her stirred me. It wasn't so much the daily care of her physical needs that moved me. It was how thoughtful she was. You see she did things for Amelia she didn't have to do. For instance, she asked Mr. Stanton to buy some pink paint so she could paint Amelia's room. Then she took one of the quilts from her own hope chest to dress up Amelia's bed. Remember the teddy bear from the first night? It had been Eileen's when she was a little girl. Her mother had bought it for her one winter when she was sick with the chickenpox. That was a true testament of her love for Amelia. I learned a lot about her when she journaled before going to bed each night.

For a while I thought that Eileen was Amelia's only ally. Then one evening I saw a side of Mr. Stanton that I admired immensely. Amelia had one of her spells where she became agitated and combative.

Eileen couldn't seem to calm her down. Mr. Stanton came in and took his little girl in his arms like you would a little baby and rocked her. Little by little she began to calm down. When she was asleep he gently laid her down on her bed and covered her up.

Then he kissed her on the forehead before leaving the room. It was such a touching moment. At that time I remember thinking why doesn't he stand up to his wife and get Amelia the help she needs. However since then I've come to appreciate that we shouldn't judge one's actions because we don't know what their journey has been.

BACK TO THE PRESENT

The couple has returned and I am so excited! You see they have opened all my windows to air me out. Oh, how good that feels. It's no longer dark and dreary inside my walls. The sun has graced me with its beautiful light. Something for which I yearned.

For the last few hours they have gone from room to room discussing my renovations. However when the gentleman suggested they go up to the third floor the woman just stood there looking up the stairs for the longest time. Then she shook her head, no, and walked away. I wish I knew for sure who she is.

I know, I know you want me to get back to the story.

Well about a year had passed since they moved in and Mr. Stanton had made quite a name for himself at work and in the community. I overheard Mrs. Stanton bragging about this to her lady friends at the weekly brunch she hosted. Although she was friendly enough, I never felt that she viewed them as her true friends but rather a means to a higher social status. This seemed to be of most importance to her. Unfortunately this was to the detriment of little Amelia.

There wasn't a day that went by that I didn't wish that someone would find out about her. Finally one day a glimmer of hope came knocking at my front door.

Eileen and Amelia were home alone that day.

When she opened the door there stood a young man in a business suit. He tipped his hat to her and said, "Good afternoon. I am Samuel Barnes with the Detroit news. I'm here to see Mr. Stanton."

"Oh, I'm sorry, but Mr. Stanton isn't at home right now."

"Well, I'm sure he'll be here soon. He asked me to meet him here."

Then he took Eileen by surprise when he knelt down and said, "Well hello, little lady. What is your name?" *Eileen turned white as a sheet when she noticed Amelia was standing there.*

She stepped in front of Amelia and said, "I'm sorry, she's a little shy."

"So is this his daughter Grace?"

Hesitating a little, Eileen said, "No, this is his niece visiting from out of town. If you don't mind I need to put her down for her nap. If you would like you may wait in the parlor for Mr. Stanton."

"Thank you so much."

"You're quite welcome."

I noticed that Samuel watched Eileen take Amelia upstairs. It wasn't until they were out of sight that he turned and headed for the parlor. From the look on his face I could tell he was quite smitten.

A little later that evening Mr. Stanton showed up at Eileen's bedroom door.

With a slightly perplexed look on his face he said, "So, Amelia is my niece now, who is visiting from out of town?"

"Oh I am so sorry, Uncle Joseph. I never meant for him to see Amelia."

"It's all right child. It was bound to happen. I hate that you had to lie, but I appreciate your discretion."

"You're welcome."

"Your aunt, being the curious sort she is, has 'graciously' invited Samuel for dinner. So I would appreciate if you would keep Amelia up here for the evening."

"That's fine. I wouldn't be good company anyway."

"Uncle Joseph, may I ask you a question?"

"Yes, you may."

"I know it's none of my business, but why don't you make some of the decisions concerning Amelia?"

"That's a good question, my dear, but it'll have to wait for another time." *Then he kissed her on the forehead and went downstairs.*

By the time he got downstairs Mrs. Stanton already had Samuel in her clutches. She seemed very interested in the article he was writing about Mr. Stanton.

"Here is your tea, Mr. Barnes."

"Thank you, but please call me Samuel."

"Well, Samuel, I was pleased to hear that you want to do a story on my husband."

"Well Mr. Stanton has made quite a name for himself and with his superb work ethic and all his charitable contributions I felt his story deserved recognition."

Standing statuesque, Mrs Stanton said ,"Well, being his wife, I'm sure you have questions for me."

"Oh Mr. Stanton covered it quite thoroughly. I believe I have all I need."

"Will you be needing a picture for your article?"

"That has been taken care of as well."

"So when will the article come out?"

"I will be presenting it to the editor- in -chief tomorrow. It will be up to him whether we will run the story and when."

"Will it be in the business section?"

"That will be up to the editor- in- chief as well."

I could tell that Mrs. Stanton was very displeased to find out that he wasn't the editor- in- chief, but she smiled nonetheless and said, "Well then, I guess we'll just have to wait and see."

Mr. Stanton seemed a bit tense and finally said, "Honey, don't you think you need to check on dinner?"

After she left Mr. Stanton apologized to Samuel for his wife's interrogation. Samuel just laughed and assured him that he was not bothered by it at all.

Then he asked him who the young woman was that answered the door earlier that day.

"That was my niece Eileen."

"Oh, is she visiting as well?"

"No, she lives with us. Her parents died a few years ago and we took her in."

"That was very kind of you."

"Well, she is a good girl, and has been a wonderful addition to our family."

"She seemed to be very nice and is quite lovely."

"Yes, she is."

"Would you mind if...."

At that moment Grace came running into the room and said, "Daddy, dinner is ready." *Then all three of them headed to the dining room.*

I was quite curious about what Samuel was going to say before being interrupted. However it became quite clear a few days later. I saw him on several occasions driving by very slowly. One afternoon when there were no cars in the driveway he stopped and came up and knocked on my door.

Eileen opened the door and being the courteous person she is, invited him in.

"I'm sorry Mr. Stanton isn't at home right now, but I'll be glad to give him a message."

With a sheepish smile he said, "Well actually, I am here to see you."

"Me? Whatever for?"

"I was hoping I could take you out to dinner sometime."

"That's very nice of you, but it's hard to get away right now because of taking care of Amelia."

"Oh, is she still visiting?"

"Yes, and will be for quite a while."

"Well, I wouldn't mind if she came along."

The smile on Eileen's face told me that she was impressed with his offer.

"That's very kind of you but I will have to discuss that with my uncle."

"How about I check back with you tomorrow?"

"That will be fine."

When Samuel left he wore a big smile and walked with a strut.

Eileen seemed pleased as well. Once she shut the door she leaned up against it and was grinning from ear to ear.

After dinner Mrs. Stanton had retired to her sitting room to read. So while the girls were playing in Amelia's room Eileen made her way to her uncle's office. She lightly tapped on the door.

"Come in."

"I'm sorry to disturb you, Uncle Joseph, but I have something I need to discuss with you."

"Alright, but please make it brief. I have a lot of paperwork this evening."

"Samuel Barnes paid me a visit today and he asked me to go out to dinner. I was wondering if that would be all right?"

"I suspected he had an interest in you. He seems to be a very nice young man. Perhaps on a Sunday afternoon when I could watch Amelia."

Eileen was so excited that she rushed over and hugged him.

"Thank you so much Uncle Joseph!"

Mr. Stanton just chuckled and said, "You're welcome. Now let me get back to work."

Eileen was practically skipping when she went back up stairs.

Later that night the Stanton's were having their nightly conversation. He informed her about Eileen's upcoming date.

With a surprised look on her face she said, "Do you think that's a good idea, Joseph?"

"I don't see why not. He is nice, clean-cut and hard-working ."

Mrs. Stanton just sat there combing her hair with a concerned look on her face. However she didn't say another word. I couldn't help but think that her only concern was that she may lose Amelia's caretaker.

The next day Eileen would periodically peek out the window in expectation of his visit. When he finally arrived she quickly ran downstairs so she could get to the door before her aunt .

When she opened the door there he stood with his hat in his hand and a big smile on his face. She smiled back and invited him to come in. Unbeknownst to her Mrs. Stanton was already striding purposely toward them.

"Well hello, Samuel, how are you doing?"

"I'm fine. How are you?"

"I'm doing quite well, thank you."

Getting to the real reason for her intrusion she said, "So what did your editor think of Joseph's story?"

"Oh, didn't Mr. Stanton tell you? We are publishing it in this Sunday's edition of the paper."

"Oh, how nice. In what section of the paper shall I look for it?"

"It's going to be on the front page. Mr. Ford insisted."

"That's very nice of him."

As she turned away to leave she added, "you make sure to tell him I said so."

Once Mrs.Stanton was out of sight, Samuel asked, "So did Mr. Stanton say you could go out with me?"

"Yes, but it would have to be on a Sunday."

With a look of hopefulness she said, "Will that be a good time for you?"

"Anytime would be a good time for me. I just want to spend some time with you."

Eileen shyly lowered her gaze and said, "That's very nice of you, Samuel."

"How about I pick you up at five?"

"That will be fine."

Then sheepishly he said, "Well I guess I better go."
He kissed her gently on the cheek and walked out
the door.

It's a good thing that no one can hear me laugh
because I was laughing really hard watching him
march down the sidewalk. Shoulders thrown back
and head held high.

When the Sunday paper finally arrived Mrs. Stanton
rushed to retrieve it. I don't believe I had ever seen
her move so fast. She quickly opened it up and
there on the front page was Mr. Stanton shaking
hands with Mr. Ford himself.

When she presented it to Mr. Stanton he dismissed
it as if it wasn't that important.

"What's wrong, Joseph? Are you displeased with
the article?"

"Oh no, it's well-written, but I'd already read it before
it went to print."

"Joseph Stanton, I've known you for a long time and there's something you're not telling me."

"Sit down, Clara."

After sitting down Mr. Stanton took her hands in his and said, "They said a lot of good things about me, for instance how charitable and kind I am."

"Oh, but you are, Joseph!"

"Well, I don't feel that way. I feel like a hypocrite. It's true I've helped a lot of people, but not my own child." Looking deep in her eyes he said, "Clara, we need to give Amelia an education."

As soon as he said that Mrs. Staton jerked her hands away and said, "We are not going to have this conversation", *then quickly left the room.*

Mr. Stanton put his head in his hand and shook it in frustration. It was then that I knew his desperation.

Although that day didn't start off well it ended quite nicely. About 3 o'clock in the afternoon Mr. Stanton came up to Amelia's room.

When she saw him her face lit up and she ran to him. He picked her up and twirled her around. She began to laugh and then wrapped her little arms tightly around his neck. It was so sweet.

Eileen was standing there laughing as she watched them interact. Smiling at Eileen he motioned for her to go get ready for her date. Then he and Amelia went downstairs.

Excitedly she entered her room, sat down at her dressing table and carefully examined the cover of a magazine. Trying to emulate the woman on the magazine, she commenced to apply her makeup. When she finished, she stared into the mirror and moved her face from side to side. After making a frustrated sigh, she got up to get dressed. I find it interesting that some humans can't see their beauty while others can't see the ugliness within their heart.

Samuel was right on time. When he knocked on the door she hurried toward the door only to have Mrs. Stanton stop her.

"Wait child, you don't want to appear anxious."

Then she inspected her to see if she looked presentable. She straightend her hair a bit and said, "Now you may answer the door."

After the pleasantries the young couple left.

I remember thinking how I wish I could leave this plot of land so I could see what happened on their date.

However when Eileen returned she told Mr. Stanton all about it.

It was about 10 o'clock when they arrived. She and Samuel lingered in the car for quite some time. Then he escorted her to my front door.

"I hope you enjoyed yourself as much as I did, Eileen."

Smiling at him she said, "Oh yes, immensely."

"We should do this again sometime."

"I would like that very much."

He gently kissed her on the cheek and waited until she was safe inside before leaving.

*Once inside she noticed that it was quiet and dark
except for a small lamp that illuminated the foot of
the stairs. She turned it off and quietly tiptoed
upstairs. When she entered the room there was Mr.
Stanton and Amelia fast asleep. She in her bed and
he in a rocking chair next to her. She just stood
there to enjoy the sweetness of it. Then she gently
nudged Mr. Stanton to awaken him.*

"I'm home, Uncle Joseph."

Slightly startled and blinking his eyes he said, "I
must've drifted off. What time is it?"

"It's a little after 10."

"So how was your evening?"

"I had a very nice time. Samuel is quite the
gentleman. He opened the door for me and even
pulled out my chair at the restaurant."

"How did that make you feel?"

"Like a lady."

Mr. Stanton grinned and said , "So where did you dine?"

"He took me to an Italian restaurant called Roma Café."

"That's a fine restaurant. What did you think of it?"

"The food was excellent, but to tell you the truth I wasn't paying much attention to the ambience."

"Oh, I see," *chuckled Mr. Stanton.* "I take it you had a good time?"

"Very much so! Afterward we strolled through the park and talked. He's quite accomplished for his age. Right after college he went to work at the Detroit news and has worked his way up to one of their top reporters."

"I know I was very impressed when he interviewed me."

"Uncle Joseph, he asked to see me again."

"What did you say?"

"I told him I would love to. Is that all right with you?"

Patting her on the hand he said, "Of course, if that's what you want."

"Thank you , Uncle Joseph."

"My pleasure, Sweetheart. *Then he kissed her on the top of her head and said,* "Now you better get some sleep."

For the next few months they saw each other quite regularly. They picnicked at the park, took long walks, and fed the ducks on the pond. I will never forget their first kiss. They were standing on my porch saying their goodbyes. Samuel looked very nervous.

While wringing his hands he finally said, "Eileen, I hope this doesn't upset you but I just can't wait any longer."

He took her in his arms and kissed her gently on the lips.

Eileen just smiled and said, "I was wondering what was taking you so long."

They both laughed and kissed one more time before she went in.

One Sunday evening the Stantons had been invited to a gathering at the Ford's home. Mrs. Stanton was ecstatic. However that didn't surprise me, she was always much happier when she was socializing with the upper crust. She even went out and purchased new outfits for her and Mr. Stanton. They looked quite elegant.

Samuel showed up shortly after the Stanton's left.

Eileen was very surprised when she opened the door and there he stood with a bouquet of flowers.

"I made arrangements with Mr. Stanton to come over and help you take care of the girls."

She pulled him inside and properly thanked him with a kiss.

*I was quite impressed with Samuel that evening.
He entertained the girls with some sleight-of-hand
tricks. They were mesmerized as they watched him
pull objects out of thin air. Then he showed Amelia
an apple and signed it to her.*

Eileen looked quizzically at him and said, "What is
that you're doing?"

"It's called sign language."

"Where did you learn that?"

"When I found out Amelia was deaf I decided to
take a class on sign language so I could teach it to
her."

*She looked at him through eyes of endearment and
said,* "That is so sweet of you Samuel."

*It was amazing how quickly Amelia caught on. She
even began bringing Samuel more objects for him
to sign to her. Both girls were so excited that it was
hard to get them to sleep.*

After the girls were finally asleep the two sat on the couch and chatted. Just as he was about to kiss her they heard someone clear their throat. When they turned around there stood the cook staring at them dispprovingly.

"Do you need something, Elizabeth?"

"No ma'am, I was just wondering if you or your gentleman friend might want something to drink?"

"No, we are fine, thank you."

Laughing, she and Samuel ran out on my front porch. After closing the door he pulled her close and passionately kissed her and said, "I love you Eileen Stanton!"

"I love you too Samuel."

I found myself smiling because not only were they the perfect couple but there was hope for Amelia after all.

Sometimes I found it hard being immobile for I longed to see what went on beyond the periphery of my vision. About every fourth Saturday Mr. Stanton would take the girls away for the day. They would leave before daybreak and wouldn't return till after dark. I often wondered what went on during those excursions. It was after those times that Amelia seemed her happiest.

BACK TO THE PRESENT

The couple who plans to inhabit me are back but this time they're not alone. There's a gentleman with them. His plaid flannel shirt coupled with a tool belt around his waist tells me he's a contractor. With pen and clipboard in hand he follows the couple around taking notes of their wishes. I'm a bit confused by one of their requests. They want each bedroom converted into two rooms. It makes me wonder just how many children does this couple have?

While the men are discussing some details the woman has left the room unnoticed. Once again she stands at the foot of the stairs that leads to my third floor. Her face is solemn. Taking a deep breath she ascends the stairs. When entering Amelia's old bedroom she surveys the room wistfully. Tears are welling up in her eyes as she walks through the rooms reflectively.

When her husband walks in and notices that she's been crying he immediately goes to console her with a hug.

Then he signs to her, "Don't worry, it will all look different once the renovations are complete."

Turning to the contractor he tells him that the wall between the two bedrooms must be removed to make one big room and each window needs to be replaced with larger plate glass windows.

That's going to be nice. There will be so much more light in the room as well as a view to my newly landscaped garden.

It's clear to me now, this is my sweet Amelia who has come home. I never thought I would see her again much less have her inhabit my walls. This makes me truly happy.

Now let's return to the story.

From the very first encounter between Samuel and Amelia, I knew he would be her godsend. Every chance he had he would teach her a few more words in sign language. That little girl was smart and she learned quickly. It wasn't long before he realized that she needed more than what little he could teach her. He expressed his concerns to Eileen one evening while they were visiting on my porch.

It was a beautiful fall evening -- My favorite time of the year. The neighborhood was arrayed with colors of red, orange, and gold. There was a slight breeze that chilled the evening air. Samuel slipped his coat over Eileen's shoulders before they sat down on my porch swing.

Eileen laid her head on his shoulder and whispered "You have been awfully quiet this evening is there something wrong?"

"No, I was just thinking about Amelia. It's amazing how fast she is learning to sign. She really needs more help than I can give her. Do you know how much longer she will be staying here?"

"Why do you ask?"

"Well, there is a school for the deaf in Detroit. They could teach her everything she needs to know to function in society."

At that moment Eileen got up and walked to the edge of my porch, and without turning around said "I'm truly touched by your affection for Amelia."

Then after a brief silence she turned to him and said, "There's something I've been wanting to tell you for a long time but didn't know if it was my place to do so. However, I love you so much that I can't hide it from you any longer. I just hope this doesn't change the way you feel about me."

Samuel walked over to Eileen, took her hand in his and said, "There is nothing you could say to change the way I feel about you."

"Well, you haven't heard what I have to say."

"Just tell me."

"Amelia isn't Uncle Joseph and Aunt Clara's niece. She's their daughter."

With a stunned look on his face Samuel said, "Then why are they telling everyone that she's their niece?"

"My aunt doesn't want anyone to know because she is afraid it will bring shame to the Stanton name."

"That's so sad."

"I know, but my uncle really wants Amelia to have an education.   So we need to tell him about the school."

"If he feels that way why hasn't he insisted on her getting an education?"

Eileen leads him back to my swing and commences to answer his question. "My aunt can be quite stubborn and temperamental. Any time he has brought up the subject she refuses to discuss it."

"Why doesn't he stand up to her."

"I've asked him the same question. He told me that
when he was a little boy his father was very abusive
to his mother. She had no say in the family. So he
swore to himself he would never treat his wife that
way. To this day he refuses to fight with aunt Clara
for fear of being like his father."

"Doesn't he care about what happens to Amelia?"

"Oh, he cares for Amelia immensely. I've witnessed
many tender moments between the two of them. In
fact every chance he gets he takes both girls out on
some land he bought. They have a picnic and
Amelia gets to play outdoors like all other children.
She loves to pick flowers and arrange them in a
basket that Uncle Joseph bought her. On several
occasions I saw tears stream down his face as he
watched her bask in the sun and twirl around in
glee. So I think we need to tell him about the
school, but we must wait till we can talk to him
alone."

*Just a few days later such an opportunity presented
itself. The Stanton's had gone out for the evening to
attend a fundraiser. After Samuel and Eileen put
the girls to bed they came downstairs to find that
Mr. Stanton had returned alone.*

"Is everything all right Uncle Joseph?"

"Yes, I just forgot my wallet and you can't go to a fundraiser without funds. I guess I'm getting a little absent-minded. I thought for sure I had put my wallet in my suit coat. It wasn't in my office. So it's got a be around here somewhere."

All three of them began looking around. Then Samuel said , "Here it Is. It must've slipped out of your coat when you picked it up."

"Uncle Joseph, before you leave, may Samuel and I talk to you about something?"

"Please make it quick, you know how impatient your aunt can be."

"Well as you know Samuel has been teaching Amelia how to sign. She is learning very quickly and we think she needs the help of a skillful teacher. Samuel found a school for the deaf in Detroit. They could teach her everything she needs to know."

Turning to Samuel Mr. Stanton said, "I appreciate the interest you have taken in my niece."

At that point Eileen with the somber look on her face interrupted. "Uncle Joseph, I told him that Amelia is your daughter."

"I see. Well Samuel I hope you haven't divulged this to anyone."

"No Sir. It wouldn't be my place to do so."

"I appreciate that."

"Here is some information about the school. I hope you'll look it over."

"Thank you. I will read over it when I have a chance."

After Mr. Stanton left, Samuel confessed, "I saw the wallet fall out of his coat. However I decided not to say anything, so when he came back to get it we could talk to him about the school."

Eileen put her hand over her mouth and giggling said, "That was quick thinking."

Then Samuel promptly added, "Shear genius, if I say so myself."

I was pleased to find out where Mr. Stanton was taking the girls on those Saturday excursions. How nice it would have been to see Amelia frolic in a field of flowers. I felt comforted that for a little while she got to feel what it was like to be a child at play. Something of which she normally was denied. This was one of the times I felt proud of being Mr. Stanton's home.

Samuel was over so much that I began to feel that I was his home as well. It was obvious that he and Eileen were very close.

One evening I found out just how close. Samuel asked Mr. Stanton if he could speak to him in private.

You know the saying "I wish I could've been a fly on the wall." Well let's just say I was glad to be the wall. Anything that went on under my roof, I had a front row seat. I had come to appreciate that although I had limitations it was important to focus on my positives.

At Mr. Stanton's suggestion they retreated to his office. After motioning for him to sit down Mr. Stanton said, "What did you want to talk to me about?"

"Well, first of all, I want to thank you for letting me be a part of your family. I've really grown close to all of you. Especially Eileen. In fact I'm in love with her. I want to ask her to be my wife. However I wanted to ask for your blessing first."

After a brief silence of contemplation Mr. Stanton said "Samuel, I believe you are a good man. So if Eileen agrees to marry you, then you both will have my blessing."

Standing up and reaching out to shake his hand Samuel said, "Thank you so much."

"You're quite welcome."

I could tell that after that part of the conversation was over Samuel seemed to relax. Then he proceeded to tell Mr. Stanton that he had gotten a raise at work and was looking for a home for Eileen and himself.

I remember wondering what kind of house he would purchase. Back then I had such a big roof that I thought no house could be as good as me. Since then I've realized that when you strip us down we are all the same.

Later that night Mrs. Stanton was sitting at her dressing table combing out her hair when Mr. Stanton entered the room.

Being the curious sort she is, Mrs. Stanton said, "What did Samuel want to talk to you about?"

"He asked for my blessing to marry Eileen."

Mrs. Stanton's shoulders dropped and she solemnly said, "I had a feeling that was coming. So when she leaves, what will we do about a caretaker for Amelia?"

"There is something I've been wanting to discuss with you concerning Amelia. There's a boarding school for the deaf in Detroit and I think we should enroll her there."

In a sarcastic tone Mrs. Stanton replied, "Oh, that is a great idea! Then when she gets out of school we can tell all our friends, "Oh by the way we have another daughter that we have been hiding away for years because she is deaf."

"You don't have to be so sarcastic, Clara."

"What do you propose we tell them?"

"I don't know. But I'm sure we can come up with a solution."

"I'm not so sure about that, Joseph. If you do this you're risking your reputation as well as your career. That's a risk I'm not willing to take."

At that point Mrs. Stanton turned back around and refused to discuss the subject any further. I felt bad for Mr. Stanton. He was so distraught that his sleep was fitful. When he left for work the next morning he looked weary.

My emotions were divided. I was sad because of the Stanton's situation, but happy for Samuel and Eileen.

As soon as Samuel got through talking with Mr. Stanton he went and told Eileen that he had somewhere special he wanted to take her Friday night, but it was a surprise.

That was another time I wish I could've left my yard. However I was front row and center when they came home that night and announced, "We are engaged."

After showing the beautiful engagement ring that graced her finger she commenced to expound on their evening.

"Samuel took me to a beautiful house in a neighborhood not far from here. When we went in the house was vacant. There was a small table and chairs in the middle of the dining room. It was elegantly set for two. Awaiting us was a chilled bottle of champagne and two flutes. He even hired a server for the evening!"

Samuel chimed in and added, "Well, I wanted it to be special."

"Oh, it was special, very special! When I picked up my napkin the ring was lying underneath it. I turned to Samuel and he was down on one knee and grinning ear to ear. Then he said the magic words."

"Eileen, although we haven't known each other for that long it has been long enough for me to know that I want to spend the rest of my life with you. Will you please do me the honor of becoming my wife?"

"I said yes before he even finished his sentence."

Eileen and Samuel both laughed and looked lovingly at each other. Then she continued, "Oh, by the way, Samuel is in the process of buying that house for us to live in."

In a cheerful tone Mr. Stanton said, "Well, I guess congratulations are in order."

Then he and Mrs. Stanton gave them both a warm hug.

All the while this was going on Amelia was standing there looking puzzled. So Samuel got down on his knees and signed to her that he and Eileen were in love. She giggled and gave him a hug.

Observing this Mrs. Stanton said, "How does she know what you were saying?"

"I've been teaching her a few words in sign language. She is very smart and is learning quickly."

"I see. I don't know if that's a good idea Samuel. We don't know sign language and we couldn't communicate with her."

"But you could learn, Aunt Clara."

Seeing that Mrs. Stanton was upset Mr. Stanton interjected, "Eileen, Why don't you and Samuel take the girls upstairs and put them to bed. Your aunt and I need to talk

Once they were out of sight Mr. Stanton took her hand and led her into his office. I could feel the tension in the air. Neither one of them sat down. Both were apprehensive as though they knew what was coming.

I enjoyed watching Mr. Stanton speak with such authority. He was kind but firm.

"Clara, I have something I want to discuss with you and I would appreciate if you would hear me out before saying anything."

Mrs. Stanton crossed her arms and curtly said, "Go ahead."

"I know you are fearful of what may happen if anyone finds out about Amelia. I understand your concerns because there will be people who will judge us. However we can't let that keep us from giving Amelia a chance for a normal life. I've seen Amelia blossom since Samuel started teaching her how to sign. The joy on her face when she understands something is priceless. We need to do this for Amelia."

"I understand what you're saying, Joseph, but what if in helping Amelia it hurts the whole family? What if we are ostracized in the community or even worse you lose your job? Then what would we do?"

"I'm sure there is a way to be discreet about this. Maybe Samuel would have some information that would be helpful. Would you please just listen to what he has to say?"

"I'll listen but I'm not sure if it will do any good."

Mr. Stanton stepped out of the room and asked the maid to tell Samuel to come to his office. When Samuel entered the room Mr. Stanton informed him of his wife's concerns.

What Samuel said next touched me deeply. "Eileen and I have been talking and I think we have come up with a solution to this delicate situation. I can enroll Amelia in school as my cousin. Then when she finishes school she can come and live with us. The house I bought isn't far from here and you can visit any time. So you'll still be a family and no one will be any the wiser."

Right away Mrs. Stanton exclaimed, "I think that is a great idea! Don't you, Joseph?"

After an awkward silence Mr. Stanton finally spoke. Putting his hand on Samuel's shoulder he said, "That's very nice of you, Samuel, but I'll have to give this some thought."

Then he left the room.

Later that night Mrs. Stanton wanted to discuss it but Mr. Stanton refused. That was one night when he and Mrs. Stanton didn't have a bedside talk. I saw worry on both of their faces.

Samuel and Eileen had decided that they would have a small wedding in my garden. I was so pleased to be a part of the happy occasion. However I was sad that my sweet Amelia would have to watch the wedding from my window.

They had arranged for the upstairs maid to sit with her.

My garden provided a beautiful backdrop for the wedding. Eileen's bouquet consisted of hydrangeas coupled with geraniums of purple and white hues. The garden gate that the Stanton's had put up the year before served well for an altar. The whole scene was quite breathtaking. The bride and groom were stunning in their wedding attire. She wore a white lace dress with a long flowing train and he a black tux topped off with a felt fedora. It was a magical moment as they declared their undying love in front of friends and family.

During the reception while the couple mingled with their guests Mr. Stanton went to check on Amelia. When she saw him she ran and jumped into his arms. I saw tears well up in his eyes. Mrs. Stanton had seen him leave and decided to follow.

"Joseph , are you okay?"

"Yes, I'm fine."

"Have you made a decision yet regarding Amelia?"

"I believe so, but I don't want to discuss it now. "

"There will be plenty of time to discuss it when they return from their honeymoon."

It was several weeks after Samuel and Eileen had returned that Mr. Stanton finally called a family meeting. After dinner the whole family adjourned to the living room. All eyes were on Mr. Stanton as he began to speak.

"First, I want to thank you all for your patience. I really had to do some soul-searching before making a decision. I'm not entirely happy with my decision but I know it's best for all those involved. I made some poor decisions when Amelia was born and now I have to suffer the consequences. However I don't want the whole family to suffer. Samuel, I have decided to take you up on your offer and let Amelia come and live with you and Eileen. I'd appreciate if you would enroll Amelia in school as soon as possible. We still want to be very involved in her life and will pay for all expenses incurred. I am truly grateful for you making this possible for Amelia."

Smiling Samuel said, "You're very welcome."

There wasn't a dry eye under my roof the day that
Amelia left for school. Samuel did his best to
communicate to her where she was going.

Although she was crying she was relatively calm.
Mr. Stanton signed to her that the whole family
loved her very much. They all embraced her for the
longest time before letting her go. Once she was
gone Mr. Stanton went into his office and wept.
Grace seemed considerably upset as well, but Mrs.
Stanton just went on about her day. I remember
hoping that staying busy was her way of dealing
with the pain.

While in school I rarely got to see Amelia. So I
eagerly anticipated the family's conversations
regarding her. Just as I suspected she was
excelling in school and all the teachers loved her.
Mr. Stanton had enrolled Grace, Mrs. Stanton, and
himself in a sign language class. He insisted that
they practiced daily. I could see the disappointment
in his eyes due to his wife's lack of effort. However,
he never gave up on her.

Weeks turned into months and months into years.
Before I knew it Amelia had blossomed into a young
woman and was about to graduate from high
school. She was the valedictorian of her class and
received a full scholarship to go to college.

One weekend when visiting she informed her parents that she wanted to be a teacher for the deaf. I thought to myself "Wow, what a noble vocation."

The family got together at Eileen and Samuel's to give her a big sendoff to college. I would've loved to see it but at least I got to hear all about it when the Stanton's had their nightly discussion.

That's when I learned a lot of things about Amelia. For instance in her second year of college she met a man named Patrick Dawson. He wasn't deaf but knew sign language quite well. He fell deeply in love with Amelia. That didn't surprise me because to know Amelia is to love her. They married shortly after they finished college.

From what I heard Patrick must've had a great sense of humor. He was quoted as saying that the reason he married Amelia was because she couldn't talk back to him. I laughed so hard that some of the shingles fell off my roof.

Patrick was studying to be a teacher as well. So after they were married the couple rented an apartment not far from the University. Patrick was hired on as a math teacher at a local elementary school while Amelia went to graduate school to be a teacher for the deaf.

I heard Mr. Stanton say that they were very happy.

Mr. Stanton was so proud of them. I was so glad that he got to see how well Amelia's life turned out before he passed away. It was so sad watching the cancer take his life. However it was comforting to see his whole family at his bedside when he took his last breath. He was loved by so many people. I heard that there were over 500 people at his funeral. He was such a good man and I was proud to have known him.

BACK TO THE PRESENT

Oh, by the way. All of my renovations are complete. Amelia and Patrick plan to move in this weekend. However they're not the only ones. There will be eight girls moving in as well. I am wearing a new plaque on my door. Engraved on it is "Stanton's School for the Deaf." I have to tell you I'm a little overwhelmed right now. I had quite an exciting afternoon.

You see when Amelia and Patrick came to inspect me for the last time they weren't alone. When Patrick came in following him was Amelia, Grace, Samuel, Eileen, and Mrs. Stanton. It was so wonderful to see everybody again. There were a lot of 'oohs' and 'awes' as they showed everyone around.

Mrs. Stanton stopped cold in front of the fireplace. As she looked up, there over the mantle was a painting of her and Mr. Stanton. She turned to Amelia and smiled. Then she signed to her, "Thank you, my daughter," and kissed her gently on the cheek.

THE END

About the author

I was born in the small rural town of Pecos Texas to Virgil and Priscilla Suttee. My father was a driller for an oil company and my mother was a homemaker. I am the youngest of seven children. Our family is really close and we all live within a few hours of each other.

My parents loved antiques and eventually Mama owned her own antique shop. Often Daddy and Mama would take us kids on what they called junk hunts. We spent hours perusing junk shops, flea markets and antique shops, looking for a rare find. On occasion we even searched for old bottles and arrowheads at abandoned homesites.

My mother was the inspiration behind this book. She was so fascinated by old houses. When she would see one she would say "look at that old house, if houses could talk oh the stories they would tell." So when I became interested in writing, I decided that I would write a book with the house telling the story of those who lived within it's walls.

My friend and mentor Mae Hoover says that all of us have a book in our head or on our heart. This book has been on my heart for over 25 years. I'm so glad to finally get it on paper. I hope you enjoy reading the stories as much as I did writing them.

Happy reading!

Lela Suttee

My stories are told by the houses in which my characters live. This book consists of three different houses telling their story. Each is quite different from the other.

First, is Elijah Sims' modest house in Texas. He built it for his beloved Sarah. Then came a tragedy that changed his life forever.

Second, is Alexander Savant's mansion in sunny California. Alexander is a musician and it appears that his only concern in life is to be rich and famous. But, when Emmy Montgomery enters his life the truth is revealed.

Third, a three story Victorian home in Michigan. It houses a well-to-do family with a big secret.

So venture back in time with the houses as they tell their story.

Lela Suttee was born in Pecos Texas. This is her first book. She is currently working on volume 2 of this series. She lives in Fort Worth, Texas with her husband and has two grown daughters and one grandson.

Email: Lela@ifhousescouldtalk.com   Website: www.ifhousescouldtalk.com

Made in the USA
San Bernardino, CA
28 February 2016